THE SHORE GIRL

Best wishes
Fran Kummel
Sept 2013

THE SHORE GIRL

A NOVEL

FRAN KIMMEL

NeWest Press

LIBRARY AND ARCHIVES CANADA CATALOGUING IN PUBLICATION
Kimmel, Fran, 1955–
The shore girl / Fran Kimmel.
ISBN 978-1-927063-17-0
I. Title.
PS8621.I548S56 2012 C813'.6 C2012-902345-0

Editor for the Board: Anne Nothof
Cover and interior design: Natalie Olsen, Kisscut Design
Author photo: Marlene Palamarek

NeWest Press acknowledges the financial support of the Alberta Multimedia Development Fund and the Edmonton Arts Council for our publishing program. We further acknowledge the financial support of the Government of Canada through the Canada Book Fund (CBF) for our publishing activities. We acknowledge the support of the Canada Council for the Arts which last year invested $24.3 million in writing and publishing throughout Canada.

NEWEST PRESS
#201, 8540–109 Street
Edmonton, Alberta T6G 1E6
780.432.9427
www.newestpress.com

No bison were harmed in the making of this book.
printed and bound in Canada 1 2 3 4 5 13 12

To my girls, Bre and Megs

REBEE

STAY ON THE BED, REBEE. AND YOU ARE NOT TO CRY.

My eyes are wet. I don't like this blanket. It's scratchy and green and I like blue. My nightie is blue with stars and the yellow moon.

Mommy went out the door. On the outside is a blinking pink light with letters and I stare at the blinking through the flower curtains but my eyes are blurry. I rub with my arm but the blurs get bigger.

I can wiggle my finger in the pillow hole and pull out the feathers and I got a pile in my hand and they feel soft like bunny's ear. I want bunny. Bunny's beside my backpack on top of the hangers. Bunny's too high. I'm not sposint get off the bed.

There are noises on the other side of the wall and they are in a party and making funny sounds with their mouth and jumping on the bed and it goes thump, thump. I want to jump up and down and make the thump, thump but I stay on the bad blanket and make the aah, aah, aah noises with my mouth. But quiet. My mouth needs a drink. Mommy says, *No more, Rebee, you'll pee the bed*, but I'm a big girl now. I go in the toilet.

The girl and the puppet went away. Now we sing pound puppy one and only puppy love. Blue is my best colour but not where you pee. I already did a pee but I didn't like the blue in the hole. *It's only coloured water, Rebee, to keep the toilet bowl clean.* And there are Kleenexes that come out of the wall and I stuck my finger in and brung a Kleenex to bed but now I can't find it in my mixed-up green blanket. I'm thirsty and I want a different Kleenex.

I don't want to sing. *The world looks mighty good to me, cause Tootsie Rolls are all I see.*

The rug is pink and some brown spills and I can see the toilet but not the blue water and not the glass with a white hat beside the soap. I can run, run, run and take off the hat and make a drink.

You do not move off this bed. You stay on the bed and wait. I'll be back soon.

I'm not sposint get off the bed. My teeth are thirsty. I can stay quiet and *stop my snivelling* and run, run, run, and make my drink and go back on the bed.

I don't like the scratchy blanket. I want Mommy to put me in my car seat with bunny. I want to drive on the highway with Mommy and see stars and cows. Where is she? I want to see Auntie Vic. I want to put barrettes in Auntie's hair, black like Snow White.

My legs don't want to run. But I got to have a drink really bad. It's a prickly rug and I don't want to step on the brown spills with my toes. Mommy forgot to turn on the light in the bathroom. I don't like the dark. It's dark in the bathroom.

I want my drink. I cover my eyes. The little table with the telephone on it bangs my tummy and my feathers are lost. My eyes are blurry and my nose too and my tummy hurts. Mommy, Mommy. *You are not to cry. You have to stay quiet.* But I can't make my snivelling stop.

I crawl on the rug and it smells like poo and I cough and my nose tickles. I'm a big girl and can get a drink by myself. My hands are on the bathroom floor, cold and sticky, and there is a black crack and a spider in the corner sleeping. *Spiders are our friends.* I'm a big girl and I climb on the toilet and I climb on the counter and I can see my yellow moon in the mirror. Hello, Rebee. Hurry, hurry, Mommy will be mad. I take the hat off and I turn the tap and it's too hard, *Try harder, Rebee*, and the water squirts out, not blue. Faster and faster. *Use two hands, Rebee, so you don't spill.* I use two hands. I want cold to drink but it's not. It's hot. It's too hot. It hurts my fingers. I don't want to let go or it will spill. I want my drink. I can't make it cold.

I cry as big as I can. The party lady bangs on the wall and yells shut up in there. *People do bad things, Rebee.* I scream louder and that's all I can hear. The water hurts. *Use two hands, so you don't spill.* But my glass falls down, down and I can't make it stop. Water splashes my moon. It's hot on my tummy. I squeeze my eyes shut so I won't see it broke.

Rattling. The door under the blinking light with letters. Mommy. I hold my breath to stop my noises but now I got hiccups. I'm not sposint get off the bed. Mommy has a key with a red board. And now the pee comes in a gush and it's hot on my legs. I pee in my nightie. And I can't breathe. My stars are all wet and there's sparkly glass, all broke, and I'm sposint stay on the bed.

And I hear her shoes coming and feel myself go up, up, and my legs drip and Mommy says, *Shuuush, baby, it's all right, I'm here.* Mommy's not mad. She turns on the light.

Mommy holds me like a baby and I'm all wet.

It's all right, Rebee.

And I lift my head off Mommy's shoulder and see her face in the mirror and she's crying. I cry some more cause Mommy's crying. Blood's coming out of her cheek. Her cheek is too big. It's blue, but not the pretty blue. Mommy looks scared.

We have to go, baby. Now.

Mommy rushes around. Clean up, clean up. She carries me to the bed and I climb out of my nightie and I smell like pee and I wrap myself up in the green blanket. I feel itchy on my belly button. Mommy sticks her candles and her black shirt and her panties in the bag with the secret pocket and she opens my backpack and pulls out my frog pyjamas and throws them at me and they land on my head. I laugh but then I see Mommy's blue cheek. *Put these on, Rebee. Hurry now.* Frog pyjamas have green feet and I can't curl my toes. I want a drink but I don't tell. Mommy drops my toothbrush in the pocket and the zipper gets stuck. Mommy is mad. Bad backpack. *Rebee, put on your pyjamas. Now.* I want my blue baby-dolls, but Mommy lifts my arms and frogs go over my head and she lifts my bum and my toes get stuck in the green feet.

A baby feather is on the green blanket. I put it in my hand. I want to tell Mommy, but she bends down and picks up the bags and a red drop from her face falls on the pink rug and she looks at that drop and a sound comes out of her mouth. She yanks on my hand too hard and I fall off the bed. I want to cry but I'm a big girl. Mommy lifts me up and we go outside under the blinky light. She throws the red key and it hits the TV and bounces on the pink rug and the door closes all by itself.

The van's got a big bash. It's all crumpled at the front like a Kleenex box when you kick it. My car seat smells like apple juice. I want a drink. I want a drink but I don't tell. *Big girls can wait.*

How did the van get broke? Mommy won't talk. Mommy is quiet. We go bump, bump, bump. There are bad noises under the van. Shaking my car seat. The trees whoosh. Then the trees go away. Fences. A big barn, maybe for chickens. Mommy's teeth chatter. Mommy's cold. I give Mommy my yellow blanket but she says no.

Turn on the lights. I can't see the cows. Mommy, turn on the lights.

The headlights are broken, Rebee. We're invisible. Lay back and close your eyes.

Mommy is sad. Are you sad, Mommy? How did the headlights get broke? How did your face get blood on it?

Go to sleep now, Rebee. Be a big girl. Close your eyes and dream about cows.

I have a feather in my hand. It's soft like bunny's ear. Bunny. Where's bunny?

Shit, shit, shit.

Can I have bunny please?

Sorry, baby, bunny's gone. We left him at the motel.

Go back. Go back. I want BUNNY!

We can't go back, Rebee. We can't ever go back.

And I cry and cry and cry.

AUNT VIC

REBEE HATES WATER. Lakes, bathtubs, alley puddles. They all scare the crap out of her. If she blames me, her dear old auntie, she's never said a word. She was only four years old and God knows what she remembers. It was supposed to be a nice surprise for the missing mommy. Look at the big girl who could float in the water. Look at the auntie who let them all drown.

Funny, the details that stick. I remember having blood in my shoe. Eddy whistling through his nose in my bed. Rebee slept on the couch in her panties and undershirt, curled into the letter C, hands over her knees. Her tiny mouth opened and closed like a little fish, like she was fighting for air in a dirty bowl.

It had been slow as a wet week at the Lucky Dollar, mostly just regulars, but the end of my left foot looked like it'd been worked over by a man with a bat. I kept telling my boss the patrons prefer a quick drink over a hobbling waitress in five-inch heels, but

Dennis, he says I couldn't go changing the uniform. I could have written the book about what Georges want, what brings a good tip, how to smell a stiff, but Dennis liked to keep his girls down, keep morale about as high as the belly of a snake.

The apartment felt sticky hot when I got home from the night shift, but I covered Rebee anyway with the old yellowed sheet she'd kicked into the couch fold. The place was a war zone. Pizza crusts and cardboard boxes, dirty napkin piles, overflowing ashtrays, a scuzzy green cup with crusties up the sides. She must have got wired pretty good. Coke float most likely, one of Eddy's two specialties, the other being pancakes with whipped topping from a can. But he'd found the book from the closet I bought for her last time. It was on the glass coffee table beside Eddy's crumpled "Skydivers, Good to the Last Drop" T-shirt, opened to Rebee's favourite, the page where Willie loses his mittens and his mother has to come rescue him. Eddy could surprise me with the things he did.

I slumped down in the chair beside Rebee's damp mop, threw my legs on the coffee table, lit a cigarette, and waited for her to wake up. Eddy was an early riser most days, too. Get him liquored up, he could miss a whole day, sleep right through and then couldn't figure out why the bank was closed, why there was no baseball from four to six like the *TV Guide* said. But there were no empties scattered about. And Eddy promised.

Eddy thought I looked like Cher and kept asking me to sing "Gypsys, Tramps & Thieves." I should have crawled into bed with him but I was too damn tired. I just sat with my feet on the pizza box and watched the blood drain from my swollen toes.

"Just a few days," Elizabeth whispered when she handed Rebee to Eddy in the middle of the night. This was a few nights before. I was doing last call at the Lucky Dollar so I missed the drop-off. But what Elizabeth said meant nothing anyway. The time before, a few days stretched to three weeks, then to three months, and when she came at last and took Rebee back, I felt a slash through my centre so deep the doctors woulda shook their heads and covered me with a plastic sheet.

Rebee whimpered. Strange little mewing sounds, like a newborn kitten crying for her mother's tit. I thought, whimper all you want, Rebee, she's not here, and even if she was, she's all dried up.

* * *

"So, how 'bout it?" Eddy asked again, pouring the bacon grease from the frying pan into his empty coffee cup.

"I can't just take off. I'll get canned."

"Not if you get a doctor's note. You get a doctor's note, they can't touch you."

"And who's going to give me a doctor's note?"

"A Doc Tor."

"For what? They give notes these days to ladies with cracked sisters who show up in the middle of the night? Leave their babies on your doorstep?"

"For your feet, that's what. You limping around like you do, they'll give you a note. Short-term disability. You and Rebee can come with me to the cabin. You can recover. Have some fun, relax."

"You live in a dump, Eddy. What are we supposed to do

while you're at work?" I'd been to Eddy's. Only once. He lived on a mountain in a shack about as big as a prison cell.

"You'll be sleeping, that's what. I'll be home for breakfast and we'll have pancakes. I'll lay down a couple hours, then we've got the whole day. We can explore the woods, do a bit a climbing."

"Well, that oughta cure my feet."

"Or whatever. I only got three more shifts anyway. Then I can pull for some time off. We can go anywhere we want, have ourselves a holiday."

"You a family man all of a sudden?"

Eddy looked wounded, but he was right. I needed some kind of plan for the kid. I couldn't just leave her alone after Eddy headed out.

So I got myself a doctor's note and fought with Dennis for a few weeks off. When I got back to the truck, Rebee was asleep, doubled over at the waist. I sidled in beside her, closed the door quietly and told Eddy it was done. I should have told him I was grateful, too, but I couldn't stand confessing to a man. So I asked him instead why I should pack up for Exshaw when my problem was fixed, for two weeks at least, and when Rebee and I could just hang out in the apartment and wait for Elizabeth to show.

Eddy didn't answer for the longest while, blowing smoke rings out his window. Rebee started to snore.

"I suppose I can't come up with a reason to suit you. 'Cause I want you to is not enough?"

"That's it? That's your big reason?"

"Whatever, Vic."

x x x

It was a dump all right. Just like I remembered.

Rebee rode up with Eddy while I followed behind in my car. No way I wanted to be stuck in Exshaw without an escape vehicle. Eddy loved listening to the big ten-fours and roger-dodgers. Rebee probably stared at the box the whole way, waiting for the voices, hugging her knees, and sucking on her finger.

The drive took forever. Eddy wouldn't give it more gas when going up a hill, and Exshaw sat on top of a mountain, the last stop. I wanted to ram into the back of him to move us along. How could she just dump her kid off with Eddy like that, a stranger to her, a guy who could be worse than the last one for all she knew?

"This is where we sleep and this is where we eat and that's where the bathroom is in case you have to go." You'd think we were in a palace or something, the way he carried on.

Rebee twirled around. "Do you got a bathtub?"

"Of course."

Eddy's place was like one of those holiday cottages that starts with a promise of good times ahead, a getaway place from the rest of your life. Only then you can't find the oomph to fix the place up, and you're left with a dump. Sure you got a mountain out your back door. But it's still a dump.

"Will you help me with the tree?" I asked him, wanting to be outside more than in.

"Don't figure we have to rush it, do you?"

"I want to get it done."

So we traipsed back out, Rebee on our heels, and headed to the truck. The mosquitoes were so thick I couldn't slap them off fast enough. Blood smears and bug guts coated my arms and legs. Eddy hopped in the back of the truck and started digging through the box. He hauled the tattered hockey flag from the bag and passed it down to me, then rooted around some more for the bungee cords and jumped back over the side.

We shuffled through the gravel, single file, to the turnoff from the highway that marked the end of Eddy's property. The highway dead-ended just up ahead. If you needed to get away from this shit piece of land, apparently you had to back out the way you came in.

"How about this one?" Eddy pointed to the tree closest to the turnoff, the tallest, its leaves choking on silver layers of filth. The cement plant chimney loomed in the distance, spewing great clouds of the stuff day and night over everything in sight.

"What you doing with the blanket?" Rebee squatted in the gravelly dip between the highway and the tree line, burying her fingers in grimy stones.

"It's not a blanket, it's a flag," I told her.

Eddy strung the bungee through the hole in the flag corner, looping it through the tree branch and pulling it tight so the flag shot up and over our heads.

Rebee watched him closely, squinting into the sun. "How come you're putting it on that tree?"

"So your mom will know where to find us," Eddy said, grunting as he hooked the bungee ends together. Then he stepped back and stood beside me, and we both looked up at the drab tattered flag, dangling lifelessly, like there was a dead body hidden beneath it.

"Mommy's coming? This morning?" Rebee sprung up out of the dirt, a load of pebbles falling from her fingers. Mosquitoes swarmed around her, chomping on her soft, pink skin.

"It's not morning, Rebee," I told her. "It's almost suppertime. Eddy's going to work pretty soon."

"Then will she come?"

"Maybe," Eddy said. I threw him a warning look but he couldn't help himself, he had this obligation to answer each of her questions. "We left her that note. On Auntie Vic's apartment door. Remember? The note tells her to look for the flag."

She looked around wildly for Elizabeth to pop out of nowhere and land in that tree. A *Slow Down, Children Playing* sign was getting ready to drop off its post. What children? And what business did they have playing on the road anyway? You'd never guess that shacks were hidden in the tangle of bushes beyond with people in them, children no less. Unless we were the only ones left.

"What if the note falls off?"

"We taped it on good. It'll stick."

Rebee held her breath, crossing her arms over her middle and squeezing. "What if a wind blows it away?"

Eddy scooped her up and pressed his fingers over hers and yanked on the bottom of the flag. "See? It's not going anywhere."

I could have killed my sister just then. "Enough already. Let's go back."

Eddy hoisted Rebee onto his shoulders and I weaved along behind them into the cabin, swatting and slapping. We fixed ourselves cheese and pickle sandwiches, and Eddy packed extra to take with him to the plant. Then we made a bed on the floor for Rebee with the blankets I brought up in the car. It wasn't fancy, but she was used to less and never seemed to notice where she got put.

"So, you gonna be all right?" Eddy asked on the way out.

It was weird, me seeing him off to work like that, Rebee underfoot, like we were an ordinary family saying ordinary goodbyes. "Sure, yah. Don't work too hard."

"Never do."

"Are you coming back?" Rebee looked at Eddy, pitifully earnest. That kid had so much coming and going in her life she couldn't trust the difference. There was nothing ordinary here.

"'Course I'm coming back," Eddy assured her. "You'll still be sleeping on that nice bed there. Then I'll make you some pancakes."

Rebee watched him go like she almost believed him.

* * *

Eddy did three nights at the plant — six to six — then he pulled some time off for what he called our "summer vacation." Some vacation. Me hobbling about, Elizabeth milling around in the back of our thoughts. Rebee kept insisting we walk down to the tree to check on the flag. She wanted to make that trip a hundred times a day. Either that, or park her butt in the dirt by the side of the road to wait.

Eddy rigged up a "build your own forest" game with an apple crate box lined with wax paper. He and Rebee kept going into the trees and coming back to the shack with as much as they could carry. Chunks of moss and rocks and twigs. Dead leaves and pinecones and other forest stuff. They arranged it all in the bottom of the crate. He got her to pretend they were angels looking down from heaven and the apple crate was their special kingdom. Only angels could see the tiny people running through the forest and swimming in the rusty old jar lid filled with water, which Eddy insisted was a lake so deep no one would ever find the bottom. Rebee kept bending over the crate, her bum in the air, and yelling, "There's one. He's a boy." Eddy told her his name was Sam. I couldn't find Sam myself, only bugs crawling and slithering and buzzing about on top of the moss.

After Rebee went to sleep that night, Eddy asked me how many kids I wanted. We'd just made love, so slow and quiet and achingly tender that I felt flushed from head to toe, like all the feelings bottled up inside me had been sucked to my skin, leaving warm purple welts of undeserved Eddy all over me. I might have cried if Rebee wasn't right there, panting her little girl sleeping breaths on the floor beside us.

He said he wanted lots. He wouldn't let it go, or me either, for that matter, wrapped so sticky tight I could hardly breathe. Eight maybe. Or ten. Girls preferably. He'd fix up an old school bus and his girls could pile in and out like every day was a church picnic.

Eddy had had enough of boys. He had six brothers, five uncles, twenty-six boy cousins and a cement plant crammed with men. Where he grew up, four shared a bed in a shabby room with a slat of a window too small to climb out of. It had a cracked concrete floor painted grey. I asked Eddy once how they did it, how they crammed themselves into that bed night after night. He said, when one got too big he just left home.

"You'll make a good mother," he whispered in the shadows. I wanted to believe him. I stayed in Eddy's arms even after they went slack, trying to match his slow, steady breaths, trying to find a place for myself inside his pretend kingdom.

* * *

By day five, there was still no sign of Elizabeth. I remember hoping she'd never come back, that she'd disappear forever. What kind of a god-awful sister wished such a thing? But we were traipsing through the trees on the deer path, the forest so thick all around that it felt like we were being woven right into it, my toes so gloriously unhurting they could break into a jog, Rebee on Eddy's shoulders, both their shorts riding low, matching bum cracks. I could have flipped through a magazine and seen this same picture, assumed it was some daddy with his little girl on his shoulders and mom following close behind, and I'd have thought it's a damn shame how some folks get to do life while others just get to see it in a magazine. It would never have occurred to me I could be that woman, stepping into this perfect moment with these carefree feet.

"Where are we going, Eddy?" I asked.

"A secret place," he called back.

"Well how far then?" I was surprised with my hardiness, the spring in my step. I wasn't even craving a smoke.

"You'll see."

The thing that made me crazy was she used to be normal. I'd be blowing smoke rings out the bedroom window, or sneaking out in the middle of the night, while she did homework or sewed curtains or put on an apron and made pudding. He was a miserable old man, our father. A circuit judge. Still is, I'm sure — miserably holding court. I haven't seen the man in nearly a decade. All those years in that house on Blueberry Hill. It should have been the sisters against the Judge, but she was so damn sweet and cheery, so damn in love with our pathetic little world that I gave up on sisterhood, packed my bags and left her behind. She was only twelve years old. I can't forgive her for that. For making me believe she'd be all right in that house.

Rebee bounced along the narrow path on top of Eddy's shoulders, her fingers wrapped in his hair. She didn't stop nattering. Eddy's a natterer, too. His best conversations were when nobody was around and he could mumble to himself uninterrupted. He'd be under his truck, plugging some leaky thing, and I'd come up beside and ask, "Who you talking to under there?" and he'd pop his head out, not the least bit embarrassed to get caught, and say, "You find company as good as mine, you can't shut up."

We made it to the end of the trail, the foot of his mountain. Eddy's kingdom was even better than the apple crate, a waterfall seeping out of the mossy rock and falling into a pool of green-blue water.

"So, whadda you think?" Eddy asked, turning quickly so he could see my face. Rebee whipped around with him, giggling. He'd been saving this moment for me, for us, and he was practically bursting to give it away. Eddy was like that. He once waited in his truck in the Lucky Dollar lot for over three hours until a break in my shift just so he could give me the silver necklace with the fairy pendant. When I opened the box and lifted the cotton, I could hear him sigh deeply, like he'd been holding the air in his lungs for hours. The fairy sits cradled naked in the slit of a moon, reaching up to a dangling pink crystal. Silver makes my skin hot and itchy, but I've been wearing it ever since.

I stepped over the smooth rocks to the edge and swished my fingers through the water. "It's our private hot tub. Only really cold."

Rebee wiggled about on Eddy's shoulders, wanting down. "Can I go swimming?" she asked, like I was her mother. "Can I?"

"It's not a swimming pool, Rebee. It's just something to look at." Eddy's eyes flashed with hurt when I said this. "And you don't even have a bathing suit," I added.

Eddy put Rebee on the ground and started to strip out of his boots, socks and jeans. "Come on, Vic. Rebee wants a swim."

Rebee tucked her arms to her sides and started to shudder, trembling in anticipation. I'd never seen her like that, wanting something that badly.

"All right, then," I bent to help her with the buckles on her sandals. "But leave your panties on. And I'm not coming in there with you."

Eddy squatted at the edge and lowered himself slowly to his waist, grimacing as he cut through the water. "Shit, it's cold," he muttered, turning towards us from the centre of the small pool, all teeth.

Rebee hopped up and down, pulling down her shorts and yanking off her top as she scuttled over the rocks. I thought she'd throw herself into the pool but she stopped abruptly at the edge.

"What's wrong, Rebee?" I asked.

Eddy stood in the water, his arms stretched wide. He was just a couple of feet away from her. "Come on, Rebee, jump. Swim to me."

Rebee backed up a step and hugged her chest.

"What's wrong with you?" I asked again. She couldn't be cold yet. Her toes were still dry. "Don't you want to go for a swim?"

"I can't swim," she said, small shoulders curling forward.

Eddy laughed. Eddy always laughed. "I'm freezing my balls off here, kiddo."

"I'm gonna drown." She said this like it was inevitable, like she could feel her lungs filling with water.

"All right. Look. I'm coming. You jump and I'll catch you." Eddy got close enough to reach up and grab her. But Rebee took another step backward, butting up against my legs.

"I'm not allowed."

When I put my hand on her bare back, she flinched. "What do you mean you're not allowed? I said you could, didn't I?"

"I'm sposint to stay on the edge," she pressed against my knees.

I whipped her around by the shoulders so that she faced me. "Did you hear me say that?"

Rebee wouldn't look at me. Eddy bobbed up and down in the background like an apple, trying to catch my eye.

"No? Well, who then? Who says you're supposed to stay on the edge?" It was cruel but I was going to make her say it anyway.

"Mommy." She wasn't moving a muscle, only the shell of her body left standing on the rock.

"Well, look around. She's not here, is she?" I pressed too hard, leaving dents on her skin, so I lowered my hands and dropped to my knees in front of her. Rebee stared at the fairy on the end of my chain. "Don't be a baby, Rebee. We're not gonna let you drown. Do you want to swim or not?"

"Come on, girl. You can do it," Eddy shouted enthusiastically behind us. "Don't leave me out here by myself. Look,

I'm a humpback whale." He fell backwards into a float, boxers ballooning with air.

"I'm not allowed," she repeated stubbornly, not even turning around to see what Eddy was up to.

"Do you want me to carry you?" I hated the thought of going in there, but I was the only aunt she had.

Rebee shook her head no, looking like she might cry. I sort of hoped she would — it's what a normal kid would have done — but she just squatted on the rock to put her legs back into her shorts.

Eddy plowed back to the edge, hoisted himself up out of the water and walked over to his clothes, leaving large wet stains on the rock.

"No big deal," he said, drying his legs with his T-shirt before lighting a smoke. He took a long drag and handed it to me, a dark look passing between us, like we'd failed her somehow. Rebee concentrated on her sandals while Eddy slid his jeans over his wet boxers. "We'll go swimming with your mom next time, Rebee," he offered. "How about that?"

Rebee slumped on the cool rock, dazedly staring at Eddy's shrinking footprints. If my sister were there I'd of drowned her myself. Not that I'd win that fight either. Elizabeth could move through the water like an eel. When the town kids got bused from school to the Chesterfield Hotel pool year after year, Elizabeth glided through the levels, miles ahead of the group. She sewed each new badge to her bathing suit, wearing them like medals. I wondered how many times Rebee was supposed to wait on the water's edge? How many times had she watched her mother slither from reach, arms dipping in and out, becoming smaller and smaller until she was nothing but a dark speck on the water's surface?

We silently retraced our steps through the winding forest trail, Eddy in front, me taking up the rear. Rebee wouldn't ride on Eddy's shoulders on the way back. A chipmunk shot past without so much as a second glance from her. I wanted to scoop her in my arms and hold her close to my breast. But I wasn't her mother. I lit a cigarette instead and kept stomping along.

* * *

I told Eddy I was heading into Canmore for a loaf of bread, but I'd have driven to South America to get a drink, to get off that mountain. And I couldn't bring the bottle back, or Eddy'd pour it down his gullet and that would be that. He wasn't a mean drunk, but he waxed philosophical and felt sorry for himself. I'd rather get punched in the ear than mop up a man's tears.

It was easy enough to find Canmore's main drag. I squeezed my rusted car into a space between two shiny BMWs and slunk along the crowded sidewalk, past the accented voices sipping wine at patio tables, past the beaded bracelets and muscular legs and sun-drenched mountain skin and the trendy little shops with flowers at their doors and crystals in their windows. I kept seeing her face. Where did she go? What happened to the girl with her once-rosy cheeks?

It didn't take long to find the right place. A real bar reeks of booze-soaked terrycloth and stale cigarettes, makes the ground tremble with its booming bass. There were no women down in that dark hole, just the hard waitress in a skimpy top, shovelling popcorn into wooden bowls from the machine in the corner. The men huddled around tables in their work boots and lumberjack shirts. They looked whipped, like they'd come straight from a shift at Eddy's cement plant. The bartender never raised an eyebrow, just bagged the bottle like I asked. I pushed up and out again into the hazy evening, and when I got to my car I started to reach in my pocket for my key but hugged my paper bag instead and kept on walking. There's a creek that winds through the town. I followed its pebbled edge for a long way, until the cheery foreigners and the mountain townspeople finally disappeared, their bubbled chatter no longer in my head. I plunked down in the grass, mountains rising around me like breasts.

I wanted to be like her once. She was easy from the day she was born, no simple feat, seeing as how her arrival brought about the end of my mother, and the end of the Judge, too, for that matter. After my mother's funeral, Mrs. Nielsen from next door took over. She was our substitute mother, a woman who cooked and sewed and doted over Elizabeth from dusk to dawn. I was four years old when Mrs. Nielsen marched into our lives, same as Rebee was then, only Rebee had a cocktail waitress for a stand-in who was piss poor at the mothering job.

Sometimes when we were little, after Mrs. Nielsen tidied the kitchen and kissed us goodbye and the Judge closed himself in his room for the night, I would climb into Elizabeth's bed. She'd give a soft squeeze first with her tiny fist and I'd squeeze back. We'd do this over and over until she fell asleep. It was clearly against the Judge's rules. We were to stay in our own beds in the room we shared. But I'd slip out from under the covers anyway once the room was dark and tiptoe across the cold floor to reach for her hand. I think she couldn't bear the loneliness of being the only one left awake in the world. Outlasting her in the dark was all she ever asked of me. That and these heartbreak Rebee stints.

I sat on the grass by the creek, the vodka going down like a friend's encouragement. You've done your best, it said. Or maybe it was Eddy I heard.

Eddy always wanted a sister. He had this romantic notion that a sister would have brought out the best in them all. The brothers could have walked her to school. Bought her dolls for Christmas. They certainly wouldn't have banged on her head until she screamed uncle, or made her stand with her arms outstretched, a stack of encyclopedias in each.

Sisters were overrated in my opinion. I'd told Eddy this, several times. Maybe he finally believed me, having met the mess that was mine. When Elizabeth stood at my door that first time, a bedraggled sixteen, I wouldn't have recognized her if she hadn't whispered my name. "Vic, it's me. Let us in." She looked hollow, haunted, like she'd been chased through the night. I took the bundle that was wrapped in her sweater, and when I pulled back the layers, I saw my niece for the first time, a scabby plucked chicken with stick arms and legs.

I knew nothing about babies. I dumped out the laundry basket and stuffed it with a cushion from the couch and laid her limp body on top, stomach down at first, but she was sucking pillow so I flipped her onto her side, and wedged her against a towel. Elizabeth collapsed on the floor beside her. I didn't have a clue what to do next so I left them like that and marched for blocks through the pouring rain to the Army & Navy. I had barely enough cash for a box of diapers. I trolled the aisles and stuffed whatever else looked right down the front of my jacket — sleepers, bibs, blankets, bottles, baby's applesauce and mashed peas. I can do this, I thought then, as I stood at the till, arms crossed, feet ready to hightail it outta there, while the lady cheerfully counted my Pampers change. Later, as I watched the two, Elizabeth staring blankly at nothing, Rebee sucking at her breast with all her concentration to try and get what she needed, I felt less sure. I told Elizabeth that I stole for her. I told her I'd do it again, as many times as it took to get us through. She pulled a fat wad of cash from her pockets and said I didn't need to bother — I owed her nothing.

It was something unspeakable. For all my trying to get Elizabeth to talk about it, she said nothing. Not of the father. Not of my father. She's stayed silent still. I've had this dream about going back to Chesterfield to break down the Judge, to hold a knife to his throat until he poured out the story, but the waking part of me can't face knowing.

The sun fell below the Canmore peaks and the creek bank filled with shadows. I drank until my insides blazed. Then I kept on drinking until I felt nothing at all.

* * *

I can't remember how I got back to the shack. If there were a God, he'd of let me crash into the cement plant.

I sacrificed the last few good swigs and chucked the bottle into the bushes before slinking inside the shack, unnoticed, vodka gurgling through my veins. Rebee and Eddy were in the bathroom, the door open a crack, their sliver of light shooting a beam through the rest of the box. I fumbled through my pockets, searching for something to chomp on to hide my boozy breath before I said my hellos. What was it exactly I'd been doing all that time? Where was the bread?

I don't know whose voices crowded into my head that night. The table lunged up, and I fell forward to hold it down with my elbows. I could hear Eddy's cooing noises and Rebee's little protests coming from the bathroom, blue blurry, as though they wheezed through the air upside down. Or maybe it was me who was upside down. The whole world had tilted. What were they doing in there? Bloodied macaroni bits swam on the plastic plate in front of my nose. I started to wretch, but forced the vodka back down.

"Come on, Rebee, quit wiggling," the slurry voice said. Where was the ketchup lid? "Stay still. Let me hold you." What were they doing in there? What was I doing out here? Something. . . . Why couldn't Eddy put lids back on? "But it hurts," the little girl cried. What was she saying? It hurts? I'm sure I heard that. What hurts? It shouldn't hurt. Hands thumped water. Hands thumped the table. "It doesn't hurt, just relax," he comforted. "Remember our deal," the man said again. "It's a secret, right," the little girl's voice. Giggling. No, no, don't giggle like that. Oh god. "That's right. You want to be a big girl," he coaxed.

Ten steps across the room, like falling down a mountain. I pushed open the bathroom door. Her pink nakedness lay out before him like an unwrapped present, Eddy kneeling, his large hand under the water.

He shot his head around, startled. "When did you get — " but I slapped the smile from his lips with a kick to his middle, and another, and another.

"What the hell?" Eddy yelled, grabbing for my foot. Rebee screamed, trying to stand, but she lost her footing and fell back in the water with an angry splash. I switched to my fists then, pounding them against his cheekbones, his ears, his throat. The shampoo bottle ricocheted against the wall and into the tub, clipping Rebee on the jaw. I pummelled Eddy harder. He hauled himself up off the edge of the tub and caught hold of my wrist and we fell sideways out of the bathroom, clawing our way across the floor, until Eddy finally straddled my middle and pinned my arms above my head.

"What the hell, Vic." Eddy was panting hard. Harder than me. A drop of blood fell from his nose to my cheek. "Jesus," he said softly. He let go of one of my hands to wipe it away and I smashed my fist into the side of his head.

Eddy pushed back from me, rocking on his knees. "Do that again you'll be sorry," he growled. He meant it. My legs were mush, my fists too, the sweat between my breasts frozen solid. I'd run out of fight.

He rolled off and stood over me, menacing, like I was a dog in need of a beating. "You're drunk, Vic."

But I wasn't drunk. Not anymore. I was a woman on the floor with a man looking down on her. "And you're a damn pervert." I couldn't meet his eyes when I said it. I was afraid I'd see just the pancake man who built kingdoms from crates.

Eddy laughed. A black sound. "I'm a pervert?"

"You had no right." He had no right to touch her.

"No right to what, Vic? Give the kid her supper. Carry her to the flag? Throw her in the tub? No right to do what?"

I wanted to curl into a ball and fall asleep and wake up far away.

"Where were you?" his boot nudged my hip, not quite a kick. "Look at me when I'm talking to you."

I pulled myself to a sit and focused on the battered table leg. How often had I left her alone with him? Three night shifts. How many coffee runs, just the two of them? That car wash. The ride up here in Eddy's truck. Asleep in Eddy's arms. Naked in the water? Where was I all those times?

"Where were you, Vic?" Eddy spoke quietly, like the question was no more than noodles for dinner. I could hear his match strike his belt buckle. "Off getting cosy with the boys in the bar?"

Off getting cosy with the kid in the tub, the voice in my head echoed back. I felt hollow inside as I clung to the table leg and crawled my way up to the smokes. My hand shook so bad it took three tries to get a flame.

Eddy's eyes were slits, the colour of cement. He raised his hand and I braced myself, but all he did was draw on his cigarette. "What exactly you accusing me of, Vic?"

What exactly was it? What did I hear? It hurts, she said. I know I heard that.

"Jesus, Vic," Eddy worked his jaw like a tooth was loose. "You're some piece of work."

"You had no right to touch her," my voice sounded so hoarse I didn't recognize it as my own. I wanted Eddy to hold me. But then the other voice in my head shot back. You let him do whatever he wanted. What was so damn important to run out on her — to leave skid marks in Eddy's dirt? Where did I throw the damn bottle?

"You think I touched Rebee?" Eddy spat. I searched his eyes for the monster, but it wasn't there. Please Eddy, make this stop.

"You really think I could do that to Rebee? Jesus, Vic." Eddy stumbled backwards. I'd never seen him look at me like that, like I was trash and the stink was unbearable. I smelled it too.

He stopped at the door to the shack waiting for me to say something. What could I say? Sorry I kicked you in the stomach. The reel in my head was so fuzzy I couldn't trust the picture. All the courage I'd felt just a moment ago drained out of me. I was an empty bottle.

"You live in the gutter, Vic." Eddy said, almost tenderly. I wanted to cover my ears.

"I suppose I can't change that," his voice quiet and measured. "Who knows what you got going on, you and that cracked sister of yours, but I'd say — " he paused, and then more quietly still, "I'd say we're about done."

I was already missing him and he hadn't even left.

"Do me a favour and don't be here when I get back. And take the kid with you." He turned and disappeared, my world slipping away, my mind seeing Rebee riding his shoulders, hanging on for dear life.

When I finally got back to her, Rebee sat shivering in the middle of the tub, hugging herself, lips blue, the water cold as iced tea. I reached for her with the towel, but she shrank back, and I had to step away to get her to climb out on her own. She stood still as a stick as I got her in her pyjamas and wrapped her in the blanket, and carried her to the car. Then I laid her in the backseat and told her to stay put while I got the rest of our stuff. The night was black as coal, so still I could hear my heart thump. I kept seeing Eddy slinking in the shadows, but it was only the trees. Eddy was gone.

She didn't make a sound as we wound our way down the mountain. I kept turning around to steal a glance at her limp body, but I was afraid I'd drive us off the road, so finally I pulled over to the side, shut off the car, and crawled in the back with her. She lay perfectly still under her blankets, fingers in her mouth, eyes huge moons against her pale skin.

"Are you okay, kiddo?" I asked, knowing she wasn't. She was biting the tips of her fingers hard, and when I reached down and pulled her hand out of her mouth, there were angry red notches just below her nails.

"Am I bad?" she asked, her voice so small I could hardly bear it.

I gathered her up in my arms and held her so fiercely she started to struggle. "Of course you're not bad, Rebee. Of course not, sweetie." What could I tell her about what Eddy had done? What had Eddy done? "Did Eddy hurt you?" I asked, making the hideous words sound matter-of-fact.

She shook her head slowly from side to side, not trusting me enough to look me in the eye. Who could blame her? She watched me try to kill the guy.

"But you said he hurt you, Rebee. You said, 'It hurts.' Remember when you said that? When you were having a bath?" Please, Rebee, please tell me I got this right.

Rebee pinched her face tightly, like she was trying to guess what I wanted to hear. I shook her a little then and she tried to bat me away. Why did I always shake her like that? I held on tighter, until her body went limp again.

"Rebee, if Eddy didn't hurt you, why did you say it hurts? I heard you say that so don't tell me you didn't." Please, Rebee, please tell me Eddy hurt you. Oh, god, what was I saying? She kept shaking her head. "You can tell me, Rebee," I pleaded. "I won't be mad." But she wouldn't say anything, so I shook her again.

"Swimmin'," she gulped. Then her eyes snapped open

and she shouted into my face, “Swimmin’ hurts. When the water goes in your ears.”

I let her go then and she scrambled out of my arms and got as far away from me as she could. She curled herself into a ball, pressed against the door handle, and dug her forehead into her blanket. I leaned against my door, straight-backed, staring into the hangover of my life. We stayed in our corners for the longest time, shallow little breaths. The windows steamed over before she finally started in with her baby snore noises. If someone had looked down on her then, you’d think she was just a little girl dreaming of pancakes for breakfast.

* * *

Eddy stopped by my apartment about a week later. I fell out of bed and limped to the door, and there he stood, hands in his pockets, rumpled and stubbly faced and so beautiful I could have fallen to my knees.

I fumbled with the chain, terrified he’d be gone before I could get the door open. But he remained where he stood, staring past me into the empty apartment.

“She’s gone,” I said when I realized what he was looking for. Rebee had clung to her mother while Elizabeth gathered up her stuff. My sister held out a roll of twenties for me, babysitting money she called it, but I told her to go screw herself. When I bent down to kiss Rebee goodbye, she wedged her face against her mother’s legs.

“Elizabeth picked her up already,” I told Eddy. It seemed like a thousand years ago.

“Just as well,” Eddy said. He had a cigarette stuck behind his ear.

After Eddy's place, Rebee wouldn't go near the bathtub. I bribed her with a packaged tea set that she could open only in the bath, but she still wouldn't climb in, not even when I made a mountain of bubbles with the dish soap. So I made her stand on a chair and chase a washcloth over her face and arms at the kitchen sink, but she moved like a robot, like the feeling part of her had died.

"I don't know where Elizabeth took her," I said weakly. Eddy just nodded.

I wanted to tell him I was sorry. That Rebee missed him. That the morning of the day her mother reappeared, I caught her with her nose in the fridge, holding the whipped topping can, doing her best to squirt a glob into her palm. She didn't hear me coming. When I laid my hand on her shoulder for comfort, hers and mine, she hurled around, and the can went whizzing across the linoleum, bashed into the cupboard, and exploded. I couldn't remember the last time I cried, and never like that. Rebee didn't step away from the open fridge door. She stood there, stone-faced, back pressed against the milk jug, and watched me writhe about on the floor, glubbing and choking and bawling my eyes out. I'll never forget her grey eyes just staring at me like that.

"Are you going to come in?" I asked Eddy, like there might still be hope. After that night at the shack, Rebee never once asked what happened to him. Never uttered his name. And here he was, at my door, Rebee long gone.

I'd not had a shower since the explosion, and I couldn't remember the last time I brushed my hair. I must have smelled like mouldy fruit, like the rotting core of all those gypsies, tramps and thieves.

"Don't think so, Vic," Eddy said finally, breaking the silence.

It took me a minute to remember my question. "So why are you here then?" The words sounded harsh, like I was accusing him again, and I bit down hard on my tongue, hoping to taste blood.

Eddy shrugged and pointed to my chest warily. I looked down at the upside-down skydiver letters. He fell out of a plane once and wanted the evidence. I'd worn nothing but for days.

I pulled the T-shirt over my head and stood naked before him, the cotton crumpled in my fist. He reached for my outstretched hand slowly, his eyes not leaving mine as he took the shirt from me. Then he backed away.

"Please stay, Eddy," I croaked.

But he just kept going.

MISS BEL

“TIME FOR SUNBURST,” I told the children. Almost every hand went up — pick me, pick me, my turn, Miss Bel!

Rebee Shore, the new girl, hid behind the other Grade Twos in the centre of the room, her nose pressed to the back of Vanessa’s sweater. She’d been here a week now. Mrs. Bagot marched down the Messenger School hallway last Tuesday afternoon, rapped on my door, announced that the girl was a transfer from the Peace River School Division, then shoved her inside. She came bedraggled, like she had rooted through a week-old hamper to pick out her clothes. Her eyes were puffy and bloodshot. I led her to the back of the class and told her to roll up her sleeves. Then I scrubbed her hands with disinfectant and wiped her face with a wet paper towel. I called Vanessa and Susan away from their desks to come join us at the sink. I told them that Rebee Shore was their new assignment, their buddy project, and that they were in charge of making her fit in. The girls moved in on Rebee like mother ducks and fawned over her like a lost lamb.

"Rebee, today you'll do Sunburst. Come."

The children separated, making way for Rebee. She inched towards me as I positioned the small chair in the greatest shaft of light pouring through the window. Vanessa and Susan took her by each arm and helped her to step up and stand on the chair. She looked condemned, head slumped, as if expecting the chair to fall and a rope to tighten and snap her neck.

"Girls, have you told Rebee about Sunburst?"

"Not yet, Miss Bel."

"All right then. Rebee, just close your eyes and stretch out your arms."

The children moved back slightly, watching Rebee closely. She was breathing fast, panting as she lifted both arms, her eyes squeezed shut. One of her shoelaces had come undone and dangled over the side of the chair.

"You're standing in a sunburst, Rebee. Does it feel warm?"

I held out my hand and clasped the tips of Rebee's fingers within mine, pushing Rebee's arm higher.

"Let the light wash over you like a warm bath. From the tips of your fingers right down to your toes."

Rebee stood a little taller, her face squeezed into one big wrinkle. She stuck out her chin, holding my fingertips tightly.

"Children, quietly now, what do you see?"

I closed my eyes, too, and listened to the children whisper their observations, just like I've taught them. The way the light danced over Rebee's face, the shine in her hair, the halo above her head, like an angel. Her sweater lighting up in stripes from the slats of the window blinds — its colour changing from red to orange. Rebee's body glowing, growing, how she became taller by standing in the light.

It's a silly game I've made up for these kids. When I opened my eyes, I saw Rebee, perched on her tiptoes, arms spread wide, like Jesus on the cross.

I wanted her to know that light doesn't hurt. "Very good, Rebee. You can open your eyes and come back to the floor."

She stepped down from the chair, tripping over her shoelace.

"Sunburst is over. Everyone to your desks."

"Should we take out our arithmetic scribblers, Miss Bel?"

"Yes, Peter. I suppose we should."

⁎ ⁎ ⁎

I chose Winter Lake for its coordinates. Longitudinally speaking, I'm now stationed at 110°00 W, directly north of the battered wooden hole, veined and stained, of the old outhouse on the farm where I was raised with the chickens. If I could find a piece of string 560 kilometres long, I could tie it to the outhouse latch, which sits on the southernmost tip of the Alberta-Saskatchewan border, run the string north along the border line, and tie it off at the Messenger School door. The outhouse still stands, although my parents have a real toilet now. It took my father six years to finish the eight-by-four room. My mother said little to hurry the process along. My mother says little during the best of times. Six years to drop a sink into the oval cutout, add a closed-in cabinet, taps to the bathtub, pipes that piped well water in and out. The bathroom door was added in year five. A doorknob to close it — year six. I was ten years old by then, but after all that waiting, the indoor toilet was reserved for visitors. My parents had the well to think about. "Water is as precious as a two-dollar bill, Belinda." To this day, the flush of a porcelain bowl makes me hear the tinkling of china, cups brought down from the back of the cupboard, teetering on saucers on the way to the table.

But it's latitude that matters the most. Latitudinally speaking, I've moved up in the world. I found the ad for my Winter Lake position while slumped in the hallway waiting for Christie to open the door. Christie and I shared a room in the dorm at the University of Regina. Having graduated already, I'd been forced to give up my key. But Christie didn't mind me hanging on. She was a big-boned farm girl who hated change, spoke only when in bed, only when her side of the room was in shadow, always with her nose pressed to the wall, always with a muffled, fluttery lisp. I had no intention of teaching like the rest of my graduating class. I was planning to go north to find my uncle. I needed more money to make the trip — I just hadn't got around to finding a job.

I was waiting for Christie, absently scanning the bulletin board across from the elevators on the dorm's sixth floor. A small slice of newsprint caught my eye. *Grade Two Teacher Reqd. Immed., Messenger Sch., Northern Lights S. D., Winter Lake.* I know my geography. The words fluttered inside like trapped swallows as I ripped the paper off its tack — *Messenger, Northern Lights, Winter Lake.* This was my winning ticket, a paid sabbatical on my journey north. Winter Lake sits at the halfway point on my climb up the provinces. From there, I can dip west and north until I hit the Welcome to the Northwest Territories sign, then traverse my way to the Beaufort Sea. Tuktoyaktuk is positioned at 69°27' N, a quarter-inch above Inuvik on page eighty-six of the *New Canadian World Atlas*. From Winter Lake, latitudinally speaking, I'll have a mere fifteen degrees to cross before I hit my mark.

So that was it, then. I waited for Christie to get off the elevator, grabbed the key from her farmer's fist, sprinted down the hallway and unlocked our door. Then I counted my escape money tucked between the covers of *Sociology in Crisis*. $321.37. Leftovers from the Rotary scholarship, my grand prize for being the student most committed. Glassy-eyed Rotarians listened closely while I read my winning essay, "An Apple for the Teacher — Passion with Purpose." Most had polished off their chocolate mousses by the time I came to the closing sentence — "And that is the weight of it, this call to the classroom, to forge a new imagination, a better world in the hearts of children." There was a great upheaval as they collectively stood in the Chamber of Commerce meeting room. Clapping and stomping. I felt light as water, as convincing as butter pecan ice cream.

I stuffed my clothes into two canvas bags, wrapped my night lights in towels and shirts: my feather-winged angel and church tower; my dead starfish; my stained glass leaf with a broken stem; and my plastic clown, whose red nose gets feverishly hot when I plug him in.

Christie wouldn't face me when I sat at her desk.

"I've got a teaching offer. In Winter Lake. I'm leaving Regina. As soon as I get these references done." I frantically pounded on her keyboard and typed three letters, designing new letterhead for each. Sincerely yours, James Knight,

Yours truly, V. Stefansson, and Best Regards, Hugh Evans: northern explorers who, despite being dead, believed in my worthiness more firmly than most.

"When did you have your interview?" Christie had her back to me and scratched at her scalp. She always scratched when she felt change coming.

"When I get there." I gathered my bags and walked out the door. "You can keep my sociology books."

I arrived at the Greyhound terminal ticket counter at a quarter to two, then waited four hours for the Winter Lake connector bus to back out of its stall. I sat in the single seat at the back, across from the toilet smells, with the reading light on. I studied my reflection in the window through the long dreary night. I'd given myself a terrible haircut. Again. My bangs were too short. My eyebrows too arching, eyes too far apart, pupils indistinguishable from irises. It took a long night of staring at myself, seven stops, one driver replacement, a nineteen-degree temperature drop, and twenty-two hours before me and my polished boots and two canvas bags lined up at the office counter of Messenger School.

"By bus? Through the night? Instead of a phone call? I've never heard such a thing." Mrs. Bagot steered me into her principal's office and pointed to the blue upholstered chair beside the plastic palm. I hadn't eaten since Regina and couldn't tear my eyes from the jar of red and green striped rock candy sitting beside the pencil holder. I had to clasp my hands together to stop them from reaching in.

Mrs. Bagot thumbed through the contents of my manila envelope. She started with my unblemished transcript. Then, the Rotary scholarship certificate on embossed paper with the gold seal. Then the sample lesson plan for contrasting simple vowel phonemes — pit, pet, pat, put, putt, pot. Last, the three reference letters.

"Those are excellent references, Mrs. Bagot. To assist you with your decision."

Mrs. Bagot breezed through the dead explorers' accolades, looking up every so often to study the girl who had garnered such praise. Mrs. Bagot later told me she was surprised by my lack of an accent, my prairie heritage, "When I appeared so, well, from so far away." I said nothing when she told me that. People smell a whiff of "difference" on me. I don't want it explained.

During my interview, I recited pieces of my Rotary essay beginning with page two and adding appropriate pauses and occasional stumbles to make it appear I was choosing my words for the first time. My mouth moved in one direction, my mind in another. I was thinking about what got me to this place. I suppose if I traced it all the way back it was that boy in the Luther cafeteria. That boy with delicate wrists, long fingers reaching into his plastic bag, pulling out orange carrots, red and yellow pepper slices, a mixture of lettuce leaves, arranging these painstakingly, as though he were a painter and his plate the palette. I sat two tables over in the noisy cafeteria, surrounded by liberal arts students I didn't know. The giant fig tree separated my table from the boy's, so I could watch without being noticed. Thick glasses magnified his worried concentration as he chewed through the colours. He had lips like a woman. He was beautiful in his otherness, so much so that he drowned out everyone else's roar until all I could hear was the sound of his breathing. When the boy stood to leave, I stood too. As he walked away, his timetable fell from the pocket of his book bag. I scooped up the crumbled paper and studied his choices. It was the first week of my second semester. By day's end, I'd switched from Arts to Education and changed all my courses to match his. If it wasn't for that boy, I might have been a sociologist. And sociology is dead — clearly.

"And I suppose that is it, this call to the classroom." Unlike the Rotarians, Mrs. Bagot neither clapped nor stomped. "My apologies for my long speech, but I feel passionate about teaching." I didn't, of course, but there are parts of a girl she must keep private, especially during an interview.

"And why Winter Lake? Why here?"

"I've been researching carefully." I knew nothing of Winter Lake other than its position on the map. "This area has an amazing history. And this school an excellent reputation."

Mrs. Bagot looked dubious. "You have no direct teaching experience."

"But I was top of my class." I felt light-headed from lack of food, sleep, light.

"And you are very young. Compared to the other teachers."

"My youth works in your favour, Mrs. Bagot."

"We've been relying on substitutes for over two months now. The children have become unruly, I'm afraid to say."

"I can fix that."

Perhaps Mrs. Bagot sensed the truth in this bit.

The next morning, after a second sleepless night, this time in the bowels of the Inn on Main Hotel, I arrived at my classroom at a quarter to nine and surveyed the thumbprint patterns etched on grimy green walls, the dishevelled stacks of cardboard along the window ledge. I routed through my predecessor's paper scraps in my top drawer.

- Cabbage and canned tomatoes (×6)
- Diet Ginger ale
- Weigh in — 4:00
- Big clothes to Jo-ann's Slightly Used
- Body Jam — 6:00 PM class

As children bounced in from the cold, I blocked the doorway to inspect each child singly. I must have gripped their shoulders too roughly. When I let go, they ran to their desks like calves after branding. With the hallway emptied, all children in, I walked first to the deep sink, scrubbed my hands, then I marched straight to the board and printed "Miss Bel" in large letters. The room was quiet as a whisper.

"Well, here we go then. We're going to clean up this dump. Scrub every inch."

* * *

My mother smacked my left hand so often with the wooden spoon those fingers still burn when they reach for a pencil. Rebee is left-handed. I love the way her fingers curl when she concentrates, smudging the letters as they inch across the page. I love the way her body stays still when she sits at her desk. She hasn't once raised her hand, joined in a discussion, or asked to go to the bathroom.

As for the others, they natter incessantly. The girls cluster like grapes; they flatter and fidget. The boys crush their juice boxes in their sweaty little fists and pound each other's foreheads and other flat surfaces.

It's a funny business, the way the mind works. I used to spend hours in my room at the farmhouse, conjuring up desks filled with breathing bodies shaped like me. I surrounded myself with girls in velvet dresses with satin sashes, boys in shirts crisp as white paper. I stole my classmates from the radio songs that drifted up from my mother's kitchen.

The real assortment is sorely disappointing. Now I find myself longing for my bedroom, away from the heat of so many grubby bodies. It's been three months now. Three paycheques, one report card, twelve Thursday after-school meetings in the teachers' lounge. There are nine green linoleum squares between my desk and the door. Sometimes I simply walk from the classroom, past the mudroom, and into the cold where I stand under the cracked canopy and suck in frigid air.

Yesterday I stood at my classroom window, inside when I was assigned to be out. It was my turn to supervise the recess raucous, but I couldn't bear another moment. Inhumane, what Mrs. Bagot expected from her teachers. I stared into the twisting, churning mass of bodies wrapped around the play equipment. A clump of girls emerged from the mouth of the vortex. It was Vanessa and Susan, and they were dragging Rebee between them, headed in my direction.

When I got to the mudroom, a blast of angry cold rushed in. Rebee stood in the open doorway between the two girls. I pulled the children inside, out of the howling entrance and slammed the door closed. Vanessa and Susan flung snow wads in every direction.

I stepped around the wet and stood in front of the drizzling trio.

"What's your problem?"

"Rebee's bin kilt," Vanessa yelled from behind her soggy

scarf. Her mittened hand pointed at Rebee's face, which was hidden by her pink scarf save for wide eyes, wet eyelashes.

"Rebee's not been killed. She's standing right here."

"See, see," Susan started giggling. Rebee stood perfectly still, eyes focused on my stomach.

"Well, let's take a look then." I stepped behind Rebee and fumbled with her scarf, the frozen knot, mutton bone hard. I was ready to give up, march into the staffroom, grab a cleaver, chop the scarf in two.

The knot finally gave, so I moved around front of Rebee and pulled the scarf from her face. Susan let out a walloping screech. Rebee's mouth was bloodied, red-caked lips forming a small doughnut, pink bubbles gathering in the hole. A blood smear had stained one cheek, her chin. Snot ran from her nose. She wouldn't look at me. Didn't cry. Didn't make a sound.

Susan's giggles turned to sobs.

"Pipe down, Susan, it's just a little blood."

I tugged and pulled and peeled the layers until Rebee was wet socks, rumpled T-shirt and baggy pants. Vanessa started shedding, too.

"Stay dressed, Vanessa. You too, Susan. Where does it hurt, Rebee?"

"In her mouth," Susan yelled.

"What happened?"

"Rebee got banged," Vanessa added.

"Banged how?"

"By Kenny's head."

Vanessa wriggled and squirmed, words tumbling like marbles in no coherent order. How Kenny pushed Rebee from behind. How Rebee lost her balance and fell. How

Rebee's mouth slammed against the curved lip of the frozen slide. How Peter laughed and pointed and the others joined in. Vanessa yakked on and on. Behind the blood splatters, Rebee, pale as a feather, still hadn't uttered a peep. Her socks were too small, heels folding at the balls of each foot.

"Leave us now. Susan and Vanessa. Both of you. Out."

They didn't want to miss the show, so I pushed them into winter and slammed the door behind them. Rebee was trembling by this point. She smelled like washing day, damp cloth, a faint trace of Christmas orange. I marched her to the bathroom and stood her in front of the sink.

"Let's get you cleaned up, then. See what we've got."

Rebee stared into the oval mirror at her blood-smeared face. She had a faraway look, as though she were looking at her older self. She was in some trailer park, some burnt-out town, some snarly boyfriend with swollen knuckles hovering in the background.

I started with the cheek. Rubbed a paper towel until the blood was all gone. Then I ran warm water over more paper, squeezed out the excess and dabbed at her chin, under her nose, around the corners of her eyes. I could see no swelling, no black and blue rising, no broken skin.

"That doesn't look so bad. Rebee, open your mouth."

Lips stayed sealed.

"Fine. Then spit into the sink for me?"

Rebee leaned over and spat a pea-sized pink plop into the sink. I still couldn't see inside her mouth. I turned on the cold water and filled one of the paper cups that sat by the tap.

"Now you take a drink and swish it all around and then spit it out. Pretend you've just brushed your teeth."

Rebee took the cup slowly, turned eyes first to me, then she swished and spat daintily onto the porcelain. Crimson fizz, then the *plink* of a little white tooth. We both leaned into the sink to get a better look.

"What is that?" she whispered.

I got a good look at the gap in the front of her mouth.

"Congratulations. You've popped your front tooth. Just like you're supposed to."

She lowered her head further, studying the tooth, poking it with her fingers. Then she turned and stared at me. Our faces were inches apart.

"Well?"

Rebee's fingers pinched my sweater. It was the first time I had really looked into her eyes. They were as grey as the end of the world, exhausted.

"Will the Tooth Fairy come?" She asked this reverently, like this might save her life.

I remembered tooth fairies and sugar plum fairies and angel fairies. Somehow, my parents had inherited a book of *Classic Fairy Tales*, a book as weighty as a fattened pig. I heaved the book onto my bed and read and reread stories of frog princes and talking cats and shoes that would not stop dancing. I waited for those fairies. They never did find their way to the middle of nowhere.

"Will she come?" Rebee asked again.

My mother had a peculiar use for lost teeth, hers and mine. She laid each on the splintered cutting board, and brought down the swinging hammer with a mighty force. Then she scooped up the specks as fine as powdered milk and fed them to her spindly geranium plant.

"What do you know about the Tooth Fairy?"

Rebee shrugged.

"What has your mother told you?"

Rebee shook her head, sadly I thought. Surely her mother had no geraniums.

"Recess must be over," I said, unwilling to drag it out further. My teacher training lacked tips for this kind of moment. "It's time to go back to the classroom."

But Rebee wanted more. "Vanessa said that when her tooth came out she put it under her pillow and she saw the tooth fairy and she had wings. The tooth fairy stayed in Vanessa's bedroom and twirled and then was gone and she got monies."

"Money. She got money."

"Does she come, Miss Bel?"

I had no decent answer. I wanted the fairy to come, my longing as sharp as Rebee's, but I had no way to find her. I yanked a paper towel from its holder, folded it twice, dug the tooth from the sink, and wrapped it snugly.

"Put this in your pocket." I passed her the tooth package. "It'll be safe there. And don't tell Vanessa. Talk to your mom instead?"

She held out her hand, opened her pocket of her pants, and tucked the paper towel as far down as it would go. I made her scrub her hands with soap and water so hot it made her eyes water. Then we marched back to the classroom, neither one of us saying a word.

It wasn't until the end of the day, after the kids were long gone, after I had disinfected my desk and stepped out into the biting wind to face the dark sky that I buried my hands deep into my coat to stop the sting. Somehow the paper towel had slipped into my pocket. I pressed my fingers around the folded square, felt the hard bump of the tiny tooth. I never thought to ask how it got there, when she might have slipped into the staffroom, chosen the exact right coat. I simply clutched that small piece of Rebee, hanging on for dear life, trying to keep it warm.

⁎ ⁎ ⁎

I live in Delta's furnished basement suite. If Delta's not the oldest living prairies teacher, I can't imagine who is. She does all her teaching sitting down and has trouble answering questions because her hearing is so poor. When I sneak past her classroom to get outside, she's often nodded off, her sixth-graders huddling over desks, speaking in low voices, like it's campfire time and the grownups have been put to bed. Mrs. Bagot has a great respect for elders. She believes in corporal punishment and checks on Delta's classroom more frequently than mine.

Mrs. Bagot made the arrangements for my stay with Delta. She marched into Delta's Grade Six classroom at the farthest corner of my wing and told her it was high time she got a new renter. Delta's last tenant, Martha Flem, collapsed from a stroke in the downstairs bathroom and got wedged between the toilet and countertop. This happened eleven years ago. Martha Flem lay there for three days, semi-conscious. Delta found her, twisted and blue with cold, her nightie bunched over swollen kneecaps. Martha must have been a large woman. I can easily sit on the floor beside the toilet, pull my knees up, and twirl a 360. She went straight to a nursing home after that, and I have to bang on Delta's upstairs door each evening and twice a day on weekends just to let her know I'm still breathing. "Delta," I yell, pounding on the door, "I'm doing just fine, no need to worry."

Often, at night, I sit on Delta's floor, my night lights glowing from every spare wall socket, bordered by overstuffed burgundy chairs, striped afghans, Royal Castle bone china girls, starched frilly doilies floating on every flat top.

I think about Buttercup, the mad dog in Delta's kitchen, locked behind baby gates. She's some kind of poodle, with matted pink curls like Delta's, a red-veined underbelly and filmy eyes. Delta has told me she needs to be put to sleep, but she can't bear to make that decision. So Buttercup chases herself in circles, round and round, always the same direction, crashing into her water bowl and garbage can. Table legs are especially problematic.

Delta went for some kind of day procedure at the woman's clinic today. A "woman's engagement" she called it, though I can't imagine her woman's parts. Delta knew she'd be late getting home and asked me to check on Buttercup. "Will you get her outside?" she asked. "Let her stand in the snow for a minute or two and take in the fresh air? She enjoys the birds, you know."

When I unlocked the door with Delta's key, Buttercup was stumbling around the kitchen, a white plastic bag wrapped tightly around her head. With each wet, wheezy intake of air, the bag moulded to the dog's head. She shook her head furiously, but it only smushed tighter. I lifted the bag away. Buttercup, drenched and panting, collapsed to the floor. But then a minute later she had turned herself around and started circling again. Like nothing had happened.

I stood naked in front of the bathroom mirror, and pulled

a plastic bag over my head. I cinched it tightly under my chin, eyelashes trapped against filmy white, the bag breathing with me, caressing my lips, and covering my tongue.

I admired Buttercup. The dog had spunk.

* * *

Rebee walks home alone each day. Vanessa and Susan, best friends forever, have since lost interest in their buddy assignment and get rides from their mothers. Rebee cuts through the schoolyard, and then hurries past the tire piles and three-legged chairs leaning in doorways, the old cars on bricks that never leave their yards. The neighbourhood has a sticky feel. Like you're walking through muck. I know this because Rebee and I take the same route until we get to the dumpster at Forrest Drive, then Rebee turns right.

Delta and I live eight blocks from the Messenger school. In a town this size, the good, the bad and the ugly are all smooshed together. Delta has bird feeders in her spruce trees, plastic deer wedged in the snow, marigolds and petunias come spring, I bet, while the guy next door chains a Rottweiler to a metal post out front.

Delta has a silver Cadillac, big enough to move into, and perches on a pillow so she can see over her steering wheel. Her feet barely reach the pedals. She offers me a ride each morning, but I prefer the walk — the neighbourhood smells and the cold on my face.

Rebee was keeping her head down, like a dog sniffing a trail, like nobody would see her if she couldn't see them. She'd made it to the dumpster, turned right. I wanted to see where she lived.

"Wait up, Rebee," I called from behind. She turned too quickly, fear in her eyes, dropping her bag in the snow.

"It's just me. Miss Bel. I'll walk with you." I bent down, picked up the bag, brushed it off, and passed it back to her. Rebee took it and kept on going, like she couldn't wait to get off the street.

"We're the new girls in town." I walked behind her. Few people had shovelled and we tried to match our footprints to those already made. Rebee's boots filled with snow. "How do you like it so far?"

Rebee shrugged. She didn't look up, the red pompom bobbing on top of her hat. She pulled down the scarf that covered her mouth so she could swipe at her runny nose.

"What do you like best?" Our breath foamed in the winter air. I puffed over her head, creating a roof that disappeared. The cold sun was so dazzling it made me squint.

"You don't talk much, do you?" She hadn't said a word to me since her tooth fell into my pocket. A tiny pink nail poked through the thumb of her mitten. "Come on. You've got to have a favourite."

"Sunburst."

"I knew it. Sunburst's my favourite, too."

We were at a corner. I hadn't walked this street before but it was more of the same — more white-laced curtains next door to unhinged shutters. Rebee looked both ways, climbed over the mountain made by the Winter Lake snowplow, and stepped out onto the street. There were no cars, no people.

We made it to the other side. She stood in front of the corner house, a dilapidated monster three storeys high, definitely more the motorcycle flag than the lacy curtains type.

Rebee leaned back and looked up, first at the top floor of the house, then at me.

"Will I get a turn again?" she asked.

"Well, I can't say for sure. Sunburst can't be decided ahead of time."

Rebee stared at me a minute, crinkling her eyes, then said, "I'm going to make juice."

"What kind?"

"Grape. Maybe."

"I'll come in with you. Purple is a good colour."

"I'm not allowed."

"Unless it's the teacher. The teacher is okay." I knew this was wrong, even as I said it. But she was so alone, so small.

We entered by a heavy cracked glass door. Inside, a mat was stacked with giant men's boots and mud-caked runners. We trudged up the steep wooden stairs, past the leftover tuna and burnt cheese smell, past the number three and four doors on the second landing, then switched directions and climbed one more flight until we got to number five. Rebee took her boots off, shaking out the snow, and placed them upside down beside the door. I did the same. Then she stripped off her mittens, hat and coat. She reached under her sweater and pulled out a key on a chain around her neck, turned the key in the lock, and we were in.

"Nobody's home," Rebee said.

"You're home," I said, dropping my coat on the floor. "You're somebody."

Rebee half-smiled. I loved the look of that bare place. The living room was a triangle, with big pillows on the floor and an electric heater inside a brick fireplace. After wading through Delta's bric-a-brac, drowning in her doilies, I felt like a sock gliding along the worn hardwood. Rebee went into the little room off the living room. I followed. It had an off-kilter look, a slanting ceiling and peeling wallpaper. None of the yellowed pansies lined up at the seams. Rebee went over to a small closet on the short side, opened the miniature door, and hung her coat on a hook, placing her bag inside. There was a foam mattress on the floor, a striped pillow with no pillowcase, and a blue blanket folded neatly on top. No chairs, no dresser.

Rebee turned, staring at me like she didn't know how I got there.

"So," I said. "Let's make us some juice."

She led me past a second small room with another foam mattress on the floor, this one blanket-heaped, with a woman's sweaters and jeans scattered about. We got to a small kitchen space. There was no window, no place for a table, just a sink full of dirty dishes, stove, and fridge. Rebee opened the fridge. Yellows, reds, greens. A half-dozen apples, two oranges, Cheez Whiz, ketchup, a paper bag, broccoli, spinach. The sociologists would have a heyday in here, call this part "fridgology," make some asinine correlation between rolling oranges and transitory lifestyles, urban alienation.

Rebee hadn't said a word.

"I lived on a farm. Not a real farm, just a few crazy chickens. We had to go outside to go to the toilet."

There was one juice can in the empty freezer and Rebee pulled it out and popped the lid off with the end of a spoon from the sink. We peered in. Only a small amount of purple concentrate stuck to the bottom of the can.

"I tried to do all my business before it got dark. Only, the more I thought about not having to go, the more I had to go, until I couldn't think about anything else."

Rebee placed the juice can on the space by the taps, reached into the dishes pile and fished out a plastic cup. She rinsed the cup in warm water. I took it from her and waited until the water steamed so I could rinse it again. Then she scooped what was left of the concentrate into the cup and filled it with cold water.

"You can have this one," she said to me, passing me the spoon and the cup with the purple sludge at the bottom. "You have to stir, mix it all through."

She'd given me the last of it. I started stirring. "So every night, I'd head to the outhouse in my pyjamas and housecoat and my outhouse boots. I waited until the last possible moment. I actually had to squeeze my legs together as I ran."

Rebee watched. She seemed intent on me getting my juice right. I kept stirring.

"I carried a big flashlight and when I got into the outhouse, I'd shine the light on the ceiling and the walls. There was a little screen on top of the wooden door, to let in fresh air I guess, but it didn't help. A hundred dead flies stuck to that screen all summer. In the winter, my dad stuck up a board piece to keep out the fresh air. That didn't help either. We can share this juice, okay?"

Rebee shook her head. "I'll have mine later. After the dishes."

I dropped my spoon in the sink and asked if we could go sit on the big pillows. My drink was lavender from top to bottom. Rebee led me into the living room, walking backwards, keeping her eye on my juice. I sat on the blue pillow and leaned against the wall under the curtainless window.

Stones of strange shapes were lined up on the windowsill above our heads. The late afternoon sun filtered in, dropping shadows on the brick mantel above the heater. Rebee pulled the green pillow close to mine, leaned against the wall beside me, her legs tucked close to her chest. The air was so dry it crackled.

"I always checked the hole no matter how bad I had to pee. I wouldn't pull down my pyjama bottoms until I shined my flashlight down the hole."

I passed my cup to Rebee. She hesitated, then took a small sip, leaving a purple film above her upper lip. She was really very pretty.

"What were you looking for? Down that hole."

I wondered if this was what it would be like to have a child of your own. To come home from work and have her waiting. She'll have stirred up some juice. When she listens to your story, she asks all the right questions.

"The craptrap monster. I thought he lived down there and waited in the dark, and if you weren't fast enough, he'd reach up and pull you down."

"Monsters aren't real, Miss Bel," Rebee shifted closer. She was holding the juice by then and she took a big drink.

"Real enough. One time, I was checking out that hole, one hand covering my nose, scared breathless 'cause of the rain. It hurt like a beating on the short run to the outhouse. Like a thousand horses pounding their hooves on me, then all around me on the outhouse roof. Just a flicker, then another, then my flashlight went dead. It was so pitch black I couldn't see the pieces of me, not the shape of my hand, not my pyjama bottoms or boot tops, certainly not the hole. But I could hear him, feel him. His waking up, his hot breath sizzling up through that hole, the rumble and creak getting louder."

"Was it the monster?" Rebee pressed further into me, our arms touching, and took another long swig.

"I think so."

Rebee squeezed her legs together and shuddered. "Did you run away?"

"I couldn't. Couldn't turn around, couldn't do anything. I was frozen to my spot on the slippery wood, leaning into the hole, peeing down my leg. Yes, that's right, Rebee. I was peeing down my leg. Eventually, I got my mouth to work. I screamed as loud as I could."

"Your mom came and got you?" Rebee looked at me hopefully.

It took me a minute to choose my ending. "No. Nobody came. My parents had the radio going and, with all that rain, they didn't hear me."

But I didn't believe what I was telling Rebee. Mom must have heard me screaming. I'd read about that queasy gut feeling a mother gets when her child is in trouble. How could she not have known?

"My mom is down by the water," Rebee said. "Probably she is."

"I finally got my legs moving and backed out of there slowly. I opened my mouth wide and screamed all the way to the house in the hammering rain, nearly drowning myself. I stayed out of the outhouse after dark from then on. I headed in its direction, so no one would suspect, then squatted behind the outhouse beside that little clump of sagebrush, which did quite well from all the attention I showered on it."

Rebee passed me the cup again and I finished the last mouthful.

"We have a inside bathroom. We always have a bathroom," Rebee said. "I hate bathtubs. Can you swim?"

"Nope. Not a stroke."

"Me either," she looked scared at the thought. "The last one didn't have hardly any hot water. It didn't come with a plug. I folded up a washcloth and put it over the hole but the water leaked out, really fast, and then there was just cold left."

"I guess those were short baths."

"Sometimes we don't have a bathtub, just a shower. That's better. This one has a — "

Someone was turning a key in the lock. Rebee jumped so quickly she lost her footing on the pillow, crashed down, and bounced back up again.

A woman with long flowing hair glided through the door, looked at me on her pillow and stood perfectly still. Mrs. Bagot would label her foreign, imported, like me. Though she was nothing like me. She was light to my dark, zero degrees latitude, a fiery heat to my north frigid zone. I felt startled by her fierce stare. The way she stood with her legs apart, arms at her side.

"My teacher is here. Miss Bel. She walked me home. She didn't ask me questions."

The woman turned to speak to the girl, who shrank back slightly. "So she was invited in, then? Oh. That's odd, because that's against the rules. You know better. What is it that she wants exactly? Why is she here?"

Her words were for me, though she stared intently at Rebee, who was looking down, pulling at the string that cinched up her sweatpants. All I wanted, exactly, was to be able to stay.

"I don't want anything, thanks," I said, uncrossing my legs, standing, stretching, sauntering towards her, my hand extended. "My name is Belinda. The kids call me Miss Bel."

She took my hand, squeezed my fingers a little too hard, and dropped her arm back to her side. From this close, she looked primordial. She was slightly taller than me, but a similar build. She had the same long limbs, same tiny wrists, same striking lack of a bosom. Her irises were ringed in amber, cat's eyes, swollen pupils, whites barely showing. Stoned-looking, but you knew she wasn't high.

"We're both new to Winter Lake. I beat you by a couple of months. Thought I'd stop in and say hello."

She took off her coat and chucked it into the room with the clothes heap. She was holding a pink and glittery pancake rock that came from her pocket. I thought she was thinking about bonking me on the head, but she didn't. Rebee ducked into the kitchen and turned on the water.

"Doing that social work teacher chore. Checking out the home. Making sure the family works," she said.

"Heavens no. Nobody can get the family to work. No, I'm not checking on anything. Not writing a report. Just popped in for some juice."

She walked over to the window and placed her stone with the others before turning to me.

"Well, thanks for popping in."

I couldn't leave. The room was murky in the fading light, hardwood dents mottling. Soon it would be dark. I walked to the window, turning so that we were both facing into the room. We leaned against the sticky windowsill, our fingertips resting on chipped paint. I swallowed the urge to wash my hands. We could see Rebee in the kitchen, perched on a stool, head bent over the sink, arms paddling through bubbly water. We stood like this, side by side.

"If I *was* writing a report, I'd give you ten stars. For your lack of crap. For renting the top floor. Spinach and grape juice."

"You've been rooting through the drawers too, Miss Bel?"

We were standing so close I could see her chest press up and down inside her black turtleneck. Mesmerizing, slow and deep. I tried to match my breathing to hers, but I was panting almost.

"You're a surprise to me." I fought with my voice to keep it low and controlled. "I walk down a Winter Lake street and stare at the windows and try to imagine the people who live behind them and how their lives go. I imagine overweight housewives with polyester tights. Painted toenails. A baby in a playpen struggling to get out. A woman with a phone to her breast, cradling it so hard I think she might shatter. I've seen all these pictures in my head. But no one like you."

"Am I supposed to be flattered? Or is this the part where I call the cops?" She pushed away from the window and from me, practically floating to the fireplace mantel. Her fingers were steady as she lit the yellow candle with matches from her jeans pocket. When she turned to face me again, her eyes reflected the glow from the candle's flame.

"I don't know how you talked my kid into letting you in. You like peeping through windows, well, here you have it. The whole enchilada." She swept her hand across the room. "You've seen it. Said your hello. Goodbye then."

Rebee was banging around in the kitchen.

"You're very rude." Six steps across the cold hardwood and I was beside her again, standing so close to the dancing flame I could feel its heat, the sulphur smell of the dead match. We stared at each other, neither backing down.

"Goodbye, Miss Bel," she said finally.

I walked slowly to the door, scooped up my coat, and left. I didn't say goodbye to Rebee. And I didn't tell her mother that I would come again.

* * *

Rebee never made it to school the next day. Or the day after that. Today, I'm about done for. I'm the kind of weary that makes the backs of your knees ache, the backs of your eyeballs sting, your tongue taste gritty, where sounds are too loud and you're jumping at nothing. I haven't slept since I met her.

Yesterday afternoon, I pulled out Rebee's file from the storage room beside Mrs. Bagot's office and memorized its checks and scribbles. Mother — Harmony Shore. Father — not applicable. Siblings — blank. Last place of residence — Peace River. Emergency contact — Victoria (Vic) Shore. Allergies — none. No medical conditions. No family doctor. All the wrong questions.

Last night I made enough light to do heart surgery by dragging two more of Delta's floor lamps into my bedroom. Usually I can keep entertained, give in to the fact that I'm the only one on the prairies who can't close her eyes for seventy-two hours straight. Sometimes I work at giving my left hand a chance. I write myself left-handed notes. Or I go through my closet, change all the hangers so my shirt buttons face the other way. Or I disinfect the floor beside the toilet where that poor woman wedged herself and polish Delta's hot water tank until it dazzles.

But last night was bad. At 3:20, I yanked on my sweatpants and hoody and boots, inserted fresh batteries into the rump of my flashlight, and snuck up the stairs, past Buttercup's door and into the night.

Winter Lake houses shrivel against the night sky like cartoon silhouettes. It's like they lose all personality after being put to bed. Except for Harmony's room, whose rock window was lit, the only one, suspended like a star. I crouched in the snow pile on the other side of the street, flashlight off, crinking my neck up, making a wish she would come to the window and give me a sign. I imagined tiptoeing up her stairs, using a key around my neck to let myself in, lying beside her, matching my breathing to hers. My feet started tingling, then numbed solid. I got so cold it felt like wolves were nipping at my wrists and at the dip in my neck. I limped back to Delta's like a cripple.

Rebee came to school this morning. She showed up twenty minutes after the bell and wouldn't look at me or the other children as she found her desk, sat, opened her practice scribbler, and picked up her pencil with her left hand. She'd kept her head down since, her cheeks the colour of cold ash.

It's quiet time. I've got the children working on *Find the Letters* worksheets from the Grade Two Teachers' Kit. Except for Peter, who thinks we should be well into phonics by now. Peter knows only how to think inside his box, to follow a set of rules he doesn't understand. He's like a woodpecker that kid, *tuttuttuttuttut*. He makes me think of my mother. I've stuck him at the back, given him the *clean the paint-brush* job.

"I want you to come into the hallway with me."

Rebee jumped. She hadn't noticed me standing beside her.

The hallway was empty. I led her to the water fountain, bent down, and let the water wash the grit off my tongue. Rebee slumped beside me, shuffling from one foot to the other.

"Take a drink. It helps. But don't touch the spout. It's got germs."

Rebee stuck her tongue out, shooting water everywhere. "Am I in trouble?" she asked, wiping her mouth with the back of her sleeve.

I leaned against the wall.

"Are you mad 'cause I missed the bell?" Rebee leaned into the wall too, the water fountain between us.

"No. I don't care about that." I wanted to give her a warm bath. I wanted to hold her head in my hand as she floated in pink bubbles. "Who's Victoria?"

"What?" Rebee scrunched her eyebrows and wrinkled her lips.

"Vic then."

"Auntie Vic."

"What's your mom's real name? Harmony. That's not it, is it?"

Rebee stayed quiet for a minute, so I gave her shoulder a squeeze.

"She used to be Elizabeth," she piped up, focusing on her scruffy runners. "But you aren't supposed to call her that. She doesn't like it."

"And where do you come from, Rebee Shore?"

She shrugged like she didn't know and then bent to yank up her sock.

"Come on, Rebee. Where? Tell me."

"I don't know the names. One time Jimmy's grandpa put Ralph on the table and cut his nails with a squeezer, and Ralph didn't like it and wouldn't wag his tail."

She picked at her sweater like it was covered with dryer lint.

"Who's Jimmy?"

She wouldn't look at me, but she kept talking at least. "He lived in the big house and we lived in the cabin. Jimmy had a monkey his grandma made with a sock his grandpa didn't wear anymore. It had button eyes but it didn't have a mouth. Then we went away so I don't know if he's got it anymore."

It surprised me to think she once had a friend. She reminded me so much of me when I was a little girl, when there were no friends for miles, no friends at all. "And where was this? Where were you living?"

Rebee shrugged again. "There's too many. Someplace."

I thought about this girl and her mother, drifting from town to town like gypsies. Who were they running from? I was about to ask, when Rebee blurted, "You're not allowed to come to my house anymore."

"Why not?"

"She said."

"Did she give a reason?"

Rebee shrugged and turned into the fountain and played with the tap. Water burped in the white bowl.

"What did she say?" I pushed off the wall, lifting her hand from the tap, and waited.

"She says you're trouble." Rebee didn't want to say this.

I could tell by her whisper, by how she addressed the water fountain. She didn't try to pull back her hand as she stared at my fingers over hers.

"What else?"

She rubbed the end of her finger against my jagged nail. I could feel it break free.

"What else?"

She wouldn't stop staring at our fingers, so I kneeled down in front of her. "What else, Rebee?"

"That if you don't stay away, we're outta here."

I took both her hands in mine and pressed them close to her chest, which gave her no place to look but my face.

"What about you?" She had eyes like her mother's, like almonds, only wider, more fearful. "Do you want me to stay away?"

I could feel her hammering heart, blood pounding through veins too small for this. Betray the mother. Betray the teacher. I wanted to protect her but didn't let myself think about what I was protecting her from. So when she shook her head no, I let go of her fists, and she fell backwards. I uncurled slowly, eclipsing her, then bowed my head and whispered in her ear. "You should listen to your mother, Rebee. Go back to your desk. And wash your hands."

She ran from me as though she'd been burned. I waited a long time before returning to the classroom. I made Peter do Sunburst, which I knew he hated. He stood on the chair, fists curled in angry balls.

I left Rebee alone until the final bell, when she could plunge into the cold and away from here.

* * *

I called in sick today. *Terrible cramps, Mrs. Bagot. The worst case of the trots. I had to call my mother in the middle of the night. Yes. Yes. Perhaps something I ate. I'll try my best. You are very kind. Ohhhhh. I must go. Thank you.*

After the morning school bell rang, I walked through back allies to the other side of town where the Safeway was. I bought a French loaf, green olives, sharp cheddar, cherry tomatoes, and slices of pink salmon — now stuffed in my backpack inside plastic bags. Then I stopped at the liquor store and bought expensive French wine from the pimply-faced boy. He talked sincerely about bouquet and body and long finishes, as though he'd travelled to France and stomped the grapes himself.

It was a cold, crisp day, no wind, a little past noon. I didn't even bother to zipper my jacket. I took off my boots in front of her door and wrapped my knuckles against wood, over and over, until she appeared.

"Hello, Elizabeth."

It frightened her that I knew her name. I could see it in her face, in the way her cheekbones shifted and her eyes narrowed, although she tried to hide it by blocking the doorway. She kept her shoulders pulled back.

"Miss Bel. No school today?"

"Thought I'd play hooky, come visit instead." She blended with her surroundings, just as I remembered. She was wearing an oversized sweatshirt, sea blue, and leggings, feet bare, her hair pulled back in a ponytail. Glasses, too, with thick black frames, a book tucked close to her chest. I had become vaguely possessive. You should always pull your hair back, I thought. Always wear blue.

"I'm not looking for company."

“But here I am. Just like that.”

I pushed past her into the beautifully bare room and heard the door bang shut behind me, feeling her cold stare on the back of my neck. I walked over to the window where she must have been reading, wrestled with the straps of my heavy backpack, and slid it to the floor at my feet. I knew she couldn’t see me, so I wrapped my fist over a rock from her shelf, bent down and slipped it into my pack.

“It’s a beautiful day. Even for Winter Lake.”

There was a striped wool blanket crumpled beside the pillow. I picked it up to feel her leftover warmth and the smell of her skin. I took the blanket in both fists, gave it a good shake, and let it billow to the floor in the centre of the room like a tablecloth.

“Tada.” I spread the wine and the food on the blanket, careful not to turn around and look into her eyes.

“I want you to go,” she told my back.

“You’re only saying that because you feel you must. Because you always do. Where’s your corkscrew?”

I headed to the kitchen without waiting for an answer, opened both drawers, and pulled out an old corkscrew, badly rusted, attached to a coil of stained rawhide. My mother would have found the dish soap, muttered and clucked. I reached for the paring knife and two plastic cups and plates from the cupboard above and carried it all to the blanket. I busied myself by fluffing up the pillows, dragging them to the blanket, opening the wine, and pouring us each a cupful.

Elizabeth still stood at the door. She had taken off her glasses and was chewing on the tip of one of its arms. I felt almost frightened by her shape in the doorway. But it was more of an aching. She could force me to leave in that moment and then it would be over.

I raised my hand, an unconditional gesture, willing some power over her.

She stood there, unmoving, while I held my breath. But then she came, sat on her pillow in cross-legged defeat, and took the cup from my outstretched hand.

"I should have brought flowers."

"Are we dating, Miss Bel?" She did not try to hide the contempt in her voice.

But I thought about it anyway, about having Elizabeth. Rebee would be with us. We'd walk together on a winter morning, sharing mittens, my hands in theirs. I was filled with a tenderness I could not explain.

"I had to sneak across town to get this stuff. Didn't want to start a Winter Lake riot for playing hooky from school. My artfulness deserves a toast. Let's drink to imports most recent, to innocence and impunity."

I touched the side of her cup with mine. We brought our cups to our lips. I could taste the freshly sawn oak and hint of vanilla, just like the boy said.

"So we're having your picnic. Are you satisfied, Miss Bel?"

"Yes, yes I am, Miss Elizabeth. Satisfied to my core."

"My name is Harmony."

"All right. I'll go with that. You call me Bel. I'll call you Harmony."

The French loaf tore under the dull knife, bread crumbs scattering over the blanket and floorboards. I wanted to borrow Delta's old Hoover, plug the cord from the lime green canister into the socket by the fireplace, and run its rumpled hose up and down along the pine planks. Elizabeth didn't notice the mess we were making. She took the bread I offered, and covered it with a slice of salmon. Then she reached for olives and tomatoes until her plate was filled.

We ate what was before us, best friends, sharing a meal. I felt pleased with my choices, colours colliding inside our cheeks.

"You don't seem the teacher type," she said at last.

"Thank God for that." My mother was a teacher. Self-appointed. We sat across from each other at the kitchen table. I perched on the Sears catalogue for the first few years, tied to the chair with a worn nylon stocking wrapped around my stomach. My mother never meant to be cruel, but she lacked imagination. The school was too far, and she knew no other way to keep a young child still. The home schooling lessons arrived in the mail like a prison sentence. *Again, Belinda. Do it again.* By Grade Five the lessons got too difficult for her. She stumbled over the reading passages and couldn't understand what the assignments were asking. I got to climb the stairs after breakfast and play school in my bedroom, tracing patterns along the window ledge in the mountains of grey dust that formed through the night. My mother never understood this principle either. She could scrub herself raw, but we lived in a dustbowl. We could never stay clean.

A crumble fell to Elizabeth's sleeve. I leaned towards her, pinched it with my fingers, and placed it on my tongue. Elizabeth failed to acknowledge my gesture. But she didn't pull away either.

"Teachers are glorified lab attendants," I continued. "The bureaucrats have clumped the kiddies together, stuck them in a Petri dish. It's the teacher type's job to stir up the mix, watch what festers. An unhygienic process, don't you think? Bad for the immune system."

She leaned back on her elbows, legs bent at the knees, her head tilted back. I imagined her at age sixty, sitting that way. She would be limber, sturdy, her beautiful neck stretched back, greying hair flowing past her shoulders.

"Then why do it? Why teach?" she stared up at the speckled ceiling like it was an open sky, where clouds in imaginative shapes wing by.

"I don't know." And I didn't really. "You get up in the morning, hard-wired to squeeze the toothpaste with the same pressure you used yesterday. Step out to wander through a day like any other."

She was still focused on the ceiling, but I could tell she was listening. "But then you press up against something that defies explanation. A man you don't recognize but already know. A woman who's drowning, so she learns to stop breathing. There is something inexplicable in the discovery. Not the discovery itself, but your connection to it. Your neural circuitry shorts out. You cross over recklessly, and in an instant, re-author yourself, start a new path. It can't be reversed."

Elizabeth laughed. I felt buoyed by the sound, its weightlessness, as though she had risen from the murky depths and floated to the surface with me. She poured herself more wine.

"It's a bullshit explanation," she said.

Her choice of words discouraged me, but I forged ahead anyway. "Can you do any better?"

"You don't like typing. You want summers off. Maybe you like kids."

"I meant *you*. Can you do any better? Explain how you

got here? Why you're sitting on this floor, in this town, with this teacher?"

"I'm sitting with the teacher because she barged through my doorway. She assumes the word 'no' doesn't apply to her."

She was not stingy with her affection. It was merely inaccessible, like a box of chocolates on a shelf too high.

"But you opened the door. And it doesn't explain the rest. How you and Rebee got to this place. The moments that led you to here. You can trace them back, you know. Try it."

She crossed her legs again, straightening her spine.

"Your one particular moment of discovery," I added. "That one connection greater than the rest."

Drops of red spread over her cheeks like food colour in water. She took another drink.

"Aren't you even going to try?"

"How I got here? The Number 2 highway, then the 55, I think. No great connections. No big moment of truth. I got tired of driving."

"So you stop when you're tired? Pick up again when you get your juice back?"

"That's about it."

"Bullshit. I don't believe it."

"I don't really care." She smiled when she said this. She looked right at me.

We sat in the fog, cross-legged, and had the rest of our picnic in silence. I emptied the last of the wine into our cups. Dregs clotted in the bottle, something the boy didn't mention. Elizabeth's eyes were shiny. She stared at the blanket.

"I'm going to live in Tuktoyaktuk," I said, trying to sound bright. We had finished our plates and I busied myself by clearing up the debris. I folded the rest of the salmon back to its bag, covered the French loaf with its plastic wrapping, carried the leftovers to the kitchen and placed them on the top shelf of the near empty fridge. We'd eaten all the olives. I threw the empty bags in the garbage and crammed them on top of the withered spinach and rotting paper. "There's enough for a snack later," I called back to her. "It's all in the fridge."

Elizabeth stood, cup in hand, and walked over to the window. "No one chooses Tuktoyaktuk." She stared at the ordinary sky covering the empty street.

"When I was a little kid my mother kept threatening to ship me there to live with the Eskimos." I dropped to my knees in front of the blanket, sweeping crumbs into my palm. "She sounded like a machine gun — *tuktuktuktuk*. I thought it was somewhere you went to be shot. Some imaginary bad place. But it's real enough. You can find it on the map."

"I suppose that explains it," Elizabeth turned to face me again. "Your lineup of moments."

Uncle Walter lived in Tuktoyaktuk. He might live there still. I wanted to tell Elizabeth his stories, stories I've told no one. About how we made magic that summer, my uncle and me.

"It's all about your mother."

"No, it's more about my uncle. My Uncle Walter."

But she'd stopped listening. "Mommy threatens. She's gonna ship you off. To Tuktoyaktuk," slurred slightly, not getting the word right. "Mommy says it over and over. Of course you're mad at Mommy. Off you go. Some kind of mad justice blowing you north."

I turned away, getting up off my knees, and headed back

to the kitchen with my palm full of breadcrumbs. "Perhaps not quite that simple," I answered, my back to her.

"Aah, but it was just a moment ago." She spoke lightly now. When I faced her, I saw she was smiling. She had her arms crossed, still holding her cup. We stood across the room from each other, she against the light of the window, me lost in the shadows. "What was it the teacher said? 'Think about the moments that led you to here. Trace them all the way back.' There we go then. You're all figured out. Let's toast the discovery. To the teacher's life. Mystery solved."

She brought her cup to her mouth, eyes glinting at me, and poured the rest of those clotted noble grapes down her throat.

I marched forward, ready to slap her cold cheek. A sting for a sting. But by the time I got to her window my fire was gone. "Life is not petty," I said. "Not yours and not mine either."

"*Tuktuktuktuk*."

"I thought you could use a friend."

"Of course you did. You're one of those people who can't see beyond her cravings. The whole world must need what you need."

"No. Not the whole world. But you and Rebee, you're not like — "

She threw her hand up then, wiping the words out of the air. "Leave us alone. Go somewhere else to find what you're looking for. There's a second-hand store down the street. Buy yourself a pretty little thing."

I couldn't stand any more, her words or mine. So I backed away from her window and walked out her door.

* * *

Delta has brought me turkey soup on a tray. A large china bowl covered with a tea towel, thickly buttered soda crackers on a little scalloped-edged dish beside, and a pitted silver soup spoon.

"Are you feeling better?" she asked when I opened the door. She was huffing heavily from her difficult descent.

"Much better, thank you. Here, let me take that. Please. Do. Come sit." I didn't like this about myself, the church voice I used around old ladies. Sing-song. Quaint. Yet I couldn't seem to stop it.

"I thought some hot soup might settle your stomach." She'd hit stormy seas on her way down the stairs. The soup sloshed everywhere, soaked the tea towel, splashing the thickly buttered crackers to a soppy mush.

"Thank you. You are very kind," my church voice said. I put the tray down on the coffee table in front of the burgundy chairs and motioned Delta to sit. She lined herself up against the closest one and dropped backwards, feet lifting into the air before thunking to the rug. I looked at the tray. Chunks of turkey ice floated in the bowl like bog bodies. An archaeological find, preserved in the depths of her freezer.

"Just look what you've done with the suite," she gazed with pleasure at her doilies and figurines, her petit point-topped stools and brocade curtains. I'd done nothing but move a few lamps and add a few nightlights. "It's just lovely."

"Thank you, Delta."

"And you keep it so tidy. Your mother must be proud."

When I left the farm for good, all my mother said was, "Don't forget to soap the can opener." Delta didn't need to know this.

"When I was your age, I enjoyed dusting too."

I did keep dusting.

"But these old bones aren't what they used to be."

"Well, I appreciate being able to borrow your vacuum cleaner," I answered pathetically.

But she was looking down, picking a bouquet of yellow fluff from her afghan. "And I'd be pleased to do the upstairs anytime at all." I raised my voice so the whole congregation could hear.

"Do you think you'll be well enough to go to school tomorrow? Mrs. Bagot has been asking about you."

For a moment I felt strangely inclined to tell the truth. To tell Delta that I was worried I might never be well enough. Delta looked right at me, ready to hear my words. I could have rested my head on her lap. Tell her how lonely I'd been. How confused. How I couldn't sleep at night. We could have talked about my new friend, a woman, a beautiful woman who was lost like me.

But the moment passed. "Oh, yes. I can't bear to miss a second day. There's so much to catch up on. I've got tomorrow's lesson still to plan. I'll be at it all night."

"Please, dear, don't let the stress of the job wear you down. You can only do your best. That's all you can do." She leaned forward, reaching for my hand.

"Such a responsibility." I leaned too, covering her warm hand in mine.

"Well, yes. It is that," she smiled at me fondly.

I smiled back. Purpled veins flattened under the pressure of my fingers.

"But you've had quite an upset and mustn't push too hard. No sense working yourself into a frenzy."

I was startled when she said this, but then I remembered we were talking stomach bugs, teaching jobs.

"I insist on driving you tomorrow. Will you let me do that at least?"

She brought me soup. I nodded.

"Good. Well, eat up. Before it gets cold."

I got Delta out of her chair with discrete little tugs and pulls, before hugging her gently at the door to my suite. Yes, most certainly, I would eat all my soup, and return the tray tomorrow when I caught a ride for school. She took the stairs, painfully slow, her grip firm on the railing, two feet to a tread before moving to the next. At the top, she turned and beamed, holding her thumb high, as though she'd already forgotten the climb. As though she were a sparkling young woman, just now returning from secrets and laughter in a rented room. Best friends forever, we could write in our diaries.

I closed my door. When I poured the soup down the sink, the shrivelled turkey chunks caught in the stopper and I dumped them in the garbage can.

I went into my bedroom, lit up my clown nose in the socket by the dresser and clicked both tri-lamps to high. I went to my drawer. Rebee's tooth was there. It lay on a bed of cotton inside a tiny gold heart-shaped container that used to hold mints. Elizabeth's rock was there too, wrapped in the folds of my favourite silk scarf. It was glittery cold stone with jagged rose edges, like an opening flower. I lay face down on my bed, that rock cutting into one fist, that tiny gold heart pressed to the other. I breathed deeply, imagining the scent of the Shore girls. But it was Delta's talcum on the comforter, her Lily of the Valley was all.

* * *

It was bannock day. Mrs Bagot had set this up. Mary Seta was in charge. Mary wore a colourful beaded dress that went down past her knees and moccasins with a quilled piece of velvet on top of the tongue. She was as old as Delta, with a deeply grooved face and soft brown eyes, a thin grey braid hanging down to her waist. Mary has had grandchildren or great-grandchildren in every grade for years and years. None of her descendants was in my class, but Mary would teach us to make bannock anyway.Mothers were everywhere. They flitted like moths around hot little bodies, straightening collars, tucking shirts into pants. The children came polished this morning, scrubbed clean. Peter wore a tie under his sweater, his mother a black dress buttoned all the way to her chin. They had identical round glasses, mother and son, and the same frozen frown. Kenny had his nose wiped and his church shoes on, shiny leather without any scuff marks. The girls wore skirts and leotards, princess and fairy sweaters, and bows in their hair. Except for Rebee, who was in yesterday's pants and black T-shirt, hair matted at the back where she hadn't thought to brush. She was prettier than the others without even trying.

Everyone seemed to know about bannock and about one another, children and mothers alike, calling out first names, laughing and jostling, milling about at their own private party. Rebee and I stood off by ourselves at separate corners of the room, watching the tumult.

Mrs. Bagot, who'd suddenly had enough, clapped her hands violently, ordering the children to go sit on the mat. The mothers gathered in a circle behind, arms crossed, a few reaching down to touch a head or shush up a child, one of their own or one of their neighbour's. I sat on top of Peter's desk, over to the side. Peter kept looking back, scowling at me, anxious I'm sure that I'd crumple his papers.

"Our people used to hunt and fish and live off the land," Mary began, her voice low and pure, nothing churchy about it. "We lived in family groups and set up both summer and winter camps, travelling between them by foot or by dog team."

Mrs. Bagot looked pleased, nodding her head as though she remembered these days.

"But that was a long time ago," Mary continued in her beautiful voice. "I was taken from my family to live at a residential school. Our land was taken away too. Stolen because of the war and the oil industry."

The mothers shuffled. Throats cleared. Everyone knew someone who worked at the weapons testing area. I wanted them all to go away, to leave me alone with Mary in a wide-open space. She could pour out the story to someone who cared about this social breakdown, a way of life lost forever. But Mrs. Bagot stepped in. The oil people were coming to the school assembly next week; it had all been arranged.

"Thank you, Mary Seta," Mrs. Bagot said. "Now, please, tell us about bannock."

Bannock, she said, was a food of her people and a taste of the north. It was a special bread of flour and lard and black currants, the dough wrapped on a long stick and cooked over a campfire until golden brown.

Kenny asked if we could have a fire. Peter said that would be against the fire regulations. Peter's mother nodded approvingly. Mary explained we would use the school stove instead. It was going to take us all morning. The first cooks were given their folded aprons, which they were to hold in their arms until they got to the kitchen. A line formed behind Mary. Off they went, children flanked on both sides by most of the mothers, Mrs. Bagot taking up the rear.

I stayed with the rest to work on our craft. The coloured construction paper had already been cut into animal shapes. Rabbits and bison, wolves and elk. I had nothing to do with it. The children were to choose an animal to decorate with felts and gluey glitter bits and then make up a Chipewyan name to write in the centre. The mothers were to help print the letters, then punch holes in both sides of the paper, which would hang on wool strings from the children's necks. We were to use only the Chipewyan names for the rest of the day.

The children ran to the craft table by the window and found chairs. Susan and Vanessa's mothers spread out the felts and poured glue blobs onto newsprint. Susan and Vanessa had been whispering on the carpet so they couldn't find two chairs together and were forced to sit on either side of Rebee.

Everyone chattered excitedly. I leaned against the window counter and let the mothers take over with their flattery and baby talk praise. "Such a pretty design, Meagan. Look what Alice has done with her colours. My, my, what happy triangles. Haven't we great artists in this room."

The children lapped up the praise like puppies at water bowls. Look at mine. See what I did. Do you like my design? All except Rebee, who kept her head down, who concentrated on drawing a jagged line in blue, then yellow, along the edge of her wolf. Vanessa and Susan leaned around her, giggling and chatting, as though Rebee were invisible and her chair empty. The mothers too. They circled Rebee, moving to the next child before bending over.

Kenny chose Feather Brain for his name, which Vanessa's mother printed for him, misspelling Brain as Brian. Vanessa was Little Rabbit. Susan asked how to spell "Buffalo Legs," which she wanted to print herself.

One by one the children chose their names, finished their decorating, and showed off the animals flapping on their chests.

"How are you, Feather Brain?"

"I'm good, Jumping Boy."

"Nice to meet you, Freckle Owl."

Rebee's wolf was the last to be done. She'd made swirls of colour, pink for the ears. When she finished her final glittery bit, she picked up the blue felt marker and painstakingly printed "REBEE" in thick, perfectly formed letters.

"You did it wrong, Rebee," Vanessa yelled.

"You got to choose an Indian name," Peter piped up.

"Too bad you used a felt marker, dear," Susan's mother wrinkled her nose at the matted hair.

"Do you want to try again dear?" Vanessa's mother said, getting all the children's attention.

The table went quiet. I could feel myself shrinking, smaller and smaller, until I was a tiny dust speck floating over the place where Rebee sat. *Again, Belinda, do it again. Do it again until you get it right.*

"I want to be Rebee." Rebee didn't take her eyes off the paper.

Vanessa's mother glared over to the window where my empty shell leaned. She thought the teacher should take charge. She didn't know the teacher had left that place, had become a floating speck in her farmhouse kitchen. A little girl tied to a chair with her mother's pantyhose.

Susan's mother leaned down to offer Rebee another paper. Rebee's cheeks went fiery red as she spread her fingers over the glitter, pressing her wolf to the table.

"There's lots more wolves," Susan's mother soothed. "I could help you make another one."

"I don't want to do it again," Rebee said, not letting go. I was floating on top of her, willing her to stay strong.

Susan's mother backed away. The children whispered and pointed. Feather Brain shouted, "Rebee's dumb," and everyone laughed.

"I only want to be Rebee," a voice so small you could hardly hear.

Vanessa leaned over and pulled at the paper under Rebee's fingers. Rebee pressed harder. The paper tore in two.

There was a collective gasp. "Oh dear," Susan's mother said. Vanessa's mother flapped her arms.

I'd had enough. I jumped back in my skin and reached for the tape, marching towards her. On the way, I kicked the back of Vanessa's chair and told her to stand up and go sit on the mat. I told the others to go too, including the mothers, and that they'd better be quiet, that I wanted it so quiet in that room I could hear my heart beat.

Rebee slumped in her little chair and I sat down beside her. I turned the wolf halves upside down, lining them up carefully and joining the tears with tape. Rebee looked up at me, then slowly flipped her paper over. It had lost some of its glitter, but unless you looked closely, you could hardly tell that the wolf had been broken. I tied the wool through the holes with double knots, slipped the string over her head, and draped her name over her heart where everyone could see. Then we stood and held hands tightly as we marched to the mat.

* * *

I woke full and warm all over. 4:17 AM. I pushed Delta's blanket away and closed my eyes, clinging to Uncle Walter before he evaporated. There, there he was. I'd found him — his soft whiskered cheeks, his drooping eye wandering every which way. I was never sure where to look as he described the northern skies, dancing with the colours of the ocean, like music. He talked about the Beaufort Sea. Of squeezed ships, crushed by polar ice, those who set sail in search of the Northwest passage and never returned. My uncle was painting the barn a ruddy red, mending our fence. I was let out of my bedroom to be his helper. Twelve years old, all limbs and longing. He told of summits shaped like cathedrals, glaciers like rivers, and walls of sculpted stone.

We had the whole summer, my uncle and me, days passing like minutes. He never stopped talking. He knew how trapped I was, how unhappy, so he gave me every story he had. A Rapunzel he called me, without her long hair. After our chores, we sat on the veranda and swatted at mosquitoes in the leftover shimmer of the sun, heat pressing down like an iron. The world came to my door with his booming laugh, like a tumbling waterfall, coating my parched lips and the dust in my throat. Even my mother cracked a smile once or twice and shed real tears when he left without warning on the twenty-fourth of August. He'd forgotten his silver eagle on a chain. I found it on the bathtub rim, hidden behind the Ajax bottle.

"Belinda, let's you and me make some light."

He suggested this on the day before he disappeared. We were in the barn and he told me to go find my flashlight. When I got back he'd pried open the trapdoor on the floor with the metal crowbar. I followed him down the rickety ladder and stood in the dirt while he reached up, pulled the trapdoor down, and closed us in. The cellar smelled at first of decay, damp earth and fermenting crabapples. After we settled in, it smelled only of my uncle, sweet tobacco and warm leather.

"We're gonna make a light show, you and me." His voice was a whispery echo. The cellar was cramped, and it was only a small light we shared. I'd never been down there and could see a few shelves looming like mountains in the night. My uncle reached into his pocket and pulled out a green roll. I held the flashlight while he unwrapped two Life Savers.

"Wintergreen. The only kind that works," he said. "Now you just suck on that for a minute. Soften it up. Whenever you're ready, just flick off the light so our eyes can adjust." We scrunched down in the tight, black wintergreen space. I flicked off the light. "You all right there, Bel? I'm right here beside you." I could hear him breathing. He was right there beside me. I didn't think to feel fear.

"Ready, now. Okay, start chewing. Keep your mouth open so we can see the show."

Our mouths shimmered and sparked. Dancing greens and blues. I expected to be shocked, some kind of jolt as my teeth sank through the layers, all crackle and flash. But light did not hurt. "Look at you, girl, you got your own Aurora

Borealis inside your mouth. Atoms ripping apart and coming together again. The same thing that makes the sky glow. In case you never get north, this'll have to do."

We finished igniting, swallowing the last tiny fragments of wintergreen. Then we scrambled up the ladder and into the glorious day.

I turned towards my uncle with breathless laughter. "Can we do it again?" I begged.

His wandering eye found mine for an instant and held. I felt so on fire, so a part of this world, I no longer recognized my body as my own. He pulled the green roll from his pocket, placed it in my damp palm. "Get yourself a little mirror. Find a dark place. Make your own light, any time you want."

I could hear Delta rumbling around upstairs. The neighbour's truck started up with a roar. The Rottweiler barked and barked. Buttercup started her frantic racing. It was 5:54. I tried to hang on, but Uncle Walter vanished, utterly, as though he might never have been.

* * *

I've missed school all week. Mrs. Bagot said that I had to get a doctor's note, that if I was not back tomorrow, she was going to dock pay. Delta slipped an envelope under my door. It was one of those all occasion cards, a Winter Lake summer shot of a girl in a rowboat. *Please get well, Belinda,* she printed in watery letters.

Elizabeth walks the snow-covered trails in the afternoons. I waited outside the dilapidated house and let her march ahead, far enough that she wouldn't turn back when she saw me. She didn't say anything when I came up beside her.

"I'm not running away," I told her. "I want you to know that."

I wanted her to know this, though I could not explain why exactly. I was not seeking approval, nor asking for permission. I needed her to know there were patterns to my life, a semblance of order. She was running from something — I was sure of that. I suppose I wanted her to think I was someone she could turn to.

The south wind was icy and I wrapped my hood tighter. Elizabeth's face was unprotected. I wished I had a scarf to give her.

"Do what you want," she said. "It makes no difference to me."

"The other day, when we were having our picnic, you said I was running from my mother."

The houses had dropped away. We reached the ravine, the forgotten place, a hint of wild in the middle of this Winter Lake town. She turned at the fork to the smaller path, and we started our descent. I fell behind her as we slid down the slippery slope.

"Remember," I yelled ahead. "You said some kind of mad justice was blowing me north. But that's not true."

"Fine," she said. "It's not true." I'd caught up again. We were in the valley, heading north. Following a frozen creek bed, ducking under branches. *Black Bear area*, the old sign said. There was barely any snow down here. No sun, just shadow. Arctic explorers, Elizabeth and I.

"I'm going north to find my Uncle Walter." Elizabeth didn't answer, didn't slow down. We passed under a ridge of rocks. Someone had painted *Fuck You Bitch* on its underbelly.

"He was a good teacher, my uncle." We were being woven into the dark forest. There was not the faintest breath of wind down there, just a reverberating stillness. If we didn't keep moving we'd be swallowed whole.

"Well, you're the teacher now. Go teach."

"I can make the Northern Lights. With my mouth." How foolish this sounded, like child's words. "I can imagine what your Uncle Walter taught you." The anger this woman brought out in me. I bit it in. "In the barn cellar."

"Figures," Elizabeth answered from some point ahead. I wanted to take the words back. To make them more notable, less sick-sounding.

I'd fallen behind again. How far had we come? Miles from the warmth of her empty room. But she was plowing through the frosted underbrush, and we were not even on a recognizable path now, circling the trees like dogs. My toes jammed against the curved end of my boot, calves aching. If only we could sit on the milk-white stones.

"Did your uncle have a good time with you?" she twisted her head backward, still marching on.

What had I said? Something about the barn cellar.

"Probably sweet-talked the whole time. Sticky little sentences. You're my best girl, aren't you, Miss Bel?"

I had one good burst left in me. I ran, six steps, seven, hit her hard from behind, pushing her against cold bark and pinning her there. She folded her arms around the sleeping aspen, forehead pressed against the tree trunk's rippling skin. I dug my boots into the mushing decay and wrapped my arms around her so our bodies draped that tree.

"Your uncle, not mine," I whispered, my mouth close to her ear. I could feel her jagged breath, the sting in her lungs. I held her pinned to the frozen tree, but I was afraid to let go, afraid of myself, those feelings.

"I don't have an uncle," she said against the rough bark. She said it matter-of-factly, as though being held prisoner was expected, nothing more than she deserved.

I wanted to tell her of that summer. That there was goodness in this world and it sparked when you found it.

"He wasn't like that," were the words I managed.

"And it's a perfect world, Belinda."

Belinda. She said my name. We untangled from each other, from the sturdy trunk that had been shoring us up, and as she turned to me her sadness turned with her like a coat made of stone.

"Go, then. Go north. Stop wasting my time." She shoved me backwards with the tips of her fingers, a push compared to my violence. Her forehead was red and swelling, three jagged scrapes, pinpricks of blood.

"I've hurt you," I said.

"Go. You don't belong here."

* * *

I am trying. Trying to do this right.

I phoned Mrs. Bagot this morning. "I'm not cut out for the classroom. You were right, Mrs. Bagot, I have too much to learn." I think she's relieved to see me leave with no fight. Vanessa's mother caught me pacing the streets when I was supposed to be on my deathbed. I waved several times as she slowed down her van. I even blew a kiss. She and the other bannock mothers must be whispering madly, beating down Mrs. Bagot's door.

Delta was harder. I spent much of last night trying to write her a letter. Page after page of false starts. Left hand, right hand, I never could get my pen to work. So this morning I picked up a single red rose and one of those blank Winter Lake cards she likes, and I simply wrote, "Goodbye, Delta. I won't forget." I placed the card and the rose on her kitchen table, along with my key. Then I waited for Buttercup to round her next corner, predictably, not like a chicken. I stopped her with my knees, scooped her up quickly and twisted her neck. I did this so quickly she couldn't have felt a thing. After she went still, I held her in my arms like a baby for the longest time. Then I filled her water dish and food bowl, gathered her little toys, mopped up her urine, and placed her lifeless body gently on the embroidered pillow I took from Delta's couch. I arranged all the toys around the pillow, then curled her into a ball to make her look as though she'd found peace and had chosen her moment to stop chasing her tail.

I know I'm not right in the head. I get confused about what's real. But there was a time when I was a little girl and my heart was pure. Elizabeth was pure once too, I'm sure of it. If she had the uncle with the wandering eye, her loveliness would light the entire sky.

Rebee's still could. She told me once, "Monsters aren't real, Miss Bel." Ever since bannock day, I've thought about how fiercely she fought against the other wolves. "This is me," her actions shouted. "I won't let you make me disappear."

I stood in the hallway of the Messenger School, well to the side of the door so the children wouldn't see. This was my last stop, possibly my last chance to do one right thing.

"I'm here for Rebee Shore," I announced when the substitute teacher answered my knock. She was very large. I wondered if those were her paper scraps in my top drawer, if she'd stopped weighing in and felt angry with herself for giving away her big clothes.

"And who might you be?"

"I might be the teacher. Miss Bel. The one you've so abundantly replaced."

"Oh. Well. Yes, then."

Rebee stepped tentatively into the hallway, obviously frightened, but then she saw me and smiled wide. I put my finger to my lips to keep her quiet until the door closed.

"Miss Bel," she whispered. "Are you going to be the teacher again?"

"Only for you, Rebee. I have something to give you before I go."

She took my hand and clung on tight as we tiptoed down the hallway. I had my other hand in my pocket, clasping two rolls of wintergreen Life Savers and the fairy mirror with the sparkly frame. We were heading to the boiler room. We'd make it black as a starless night before we burst into light.

REBEE

SOME MOTHERS CHEW THE ENDS OF THEIR BABIES' FINGERS AND SPIT OUT THE NAILS. This keeps the babies from scratching their noses and cheeks when they bat their fists at nothing. I asked my mother if she did that for me. She looked out the window and said I should ask about French kissing or rosebud tattoos like normal girls.

If you're left-handed, the fingernails on your left hand grow faster. Visa-versa for right-handers. When people die, their fingernails keep growing after they're buried in the ground. Toenails too. They grow straight, like daggers. When they run out of room in the coffin, they curl and loop like roots.

I don't use my left hand much anymore. My fingers must be confused. All my nails are stubby dead ends. They stopped growing after being hammered by a volleyball. When gym class was over, my first finger drooped at the knuckle like a candy cane. I could pull it straight, but when I let go, it curled back under. Mallet finger, the school nurse called it. She told me to get it splinted at the hospital. Said I'd be right as rain in six short weeks.

Mom doesn't believe in hospitals. *Does it hurt, Rebee?* she asked. *Look at that, like pokin' a caterpillar.* She laughed and said I could point at people, and they'd never know. I tried a Popsicle stick and Scotch tape, but my finger just turned purple. When the Scotch tape ran out, I gave up.

I can't button shirts or pick up a jellybean with a floppy finger that has no feeling. But if I rest my left hand against my coat sleeve or desktop, it almost looks normal.

¥ ¥ ¥

I collect nail clippings and keep them in a plastic box that used to hold elastics. Nobody knows.

My nails come from all over. Most are my mother's. She calls herself Harmony. Harmony leaves the slivers lying in the tub. I come along afterwards, scoop them up and drop them in the plastic box. Passion purple pinky trimmings from the lousy bed hotel. Carstairs. Sparkly red glitter bits from the place with ceilings that peed when it rained. Fort McMurray I think. I've picked up a few from the floor of the van. Harmony could do without shoes year round if her toes wouldn't fall off in the snow. I read somewhere that it's illegal to drive in bare feet. When I told this to her, she said, "So hand me over, Rebee. Here's your chance."

At my Aunt Vic's place I saw on *Ripley's Believe It or Not* the old man from Bangkok with the longest fingernails in the world. Over twenty feet of nails. His one hand had five golden twisted ropes that dragged the floor and curved back up again like a ram's horns. He couldn't ride a bike, turn pages of a book, or sleep through the night. He tried to sell them for $20,000, but nobody wanted nails. If I had the money, I'd buy them in a flash. Nails are like magic. Roll someone's nail between your fingers, it brings back a slice of somewhere you've been. A whisper, the smell of oranges, fridge noises. Somewhere forgotten, but it's out there somewhere.

* * *

We move around a lot. Harmony gets restless. For her, a new place has a three-month expiry date, same as fruit bars. Harmony loves moving day. She skips between rooms, pink cheeked, eyes glowing with the thought of waking in a place where she has to hunt for the light switch. She collects her candles, crystals, incense sticks, her bear claws and peacock feathers, creates a pile on top of the Indian sari we use for a tablecloth, and folds it like a diaper.

We roll foamies and quilts. Stuff our clothes into green garbage bags. Fill cardboard boxes with our garage sale dishes and mismatched cutlery, half-empty jars of mayo and peanut butter. Harmony laughs as we struggle onto the street with the giant blue pillows, the folding wooden table and old chairs, the ghetto blaster and the rest. Everything we own fits in the white van.

My stuff goes into a bag I keep at my feet. My toothbrush and Walkman, jalapeno chips and Sour Pusses, my sparkly mirror and my nail clipping box.

We arrange ourselves on the front seat. Be a doll, Rebee, quit smacking your gum. She places her sugared coffee in its holder beside mine. I pull out my Walkman and plug myself in. *Shake it down ladies. Make this your night. Be free, uh-uh, be free. Are you ready?*

I flick the tip of my bad finger against my zipper pull and watch it flop like a fish. I stare at my fingertips. At least I won't be like the Oklahoma nurses. The nurses cuddled the sickly babies, changed their diapers, fed them warm milk, loved 'em to death. All that bacteria festering under their long, shiny nails. When I have babies, I'll nurse on their curled fists and hold their slivers in my mouth — tiny white slivers. One at a time.

We rumble along the highway under a watery sky, past wheat rolled into giant soup cans, cows frozen in muck. I think about where we just came from. I can't remember the colour of the walls or feel of the curtains or shape of the bathroom sink. Blank as water, like on a test day in a new school and I end up at the fountain, gulping, drowning.

I slip off my runners and slide my toe across my bag until it touches my nail box.

We'll get to wherever we're going tonight. Unload the white van. Light an incense stick. Find the little hidey spots.

Harmony will crash, a smile on her lips.

I'll wait awhile. Sprinkle the brittle bits on my blanket. Sift them like seashells.

JAKE

I CAME TO, GULPING, CLUTCHING MY RIBS, opened the eye not nailed to the table, and stared blearily through the empty Jack Daniel's bottle. I tried to think, to find one quiet body part. I rolled my ankles in circles, right, then left.

After several minutes I unfolded and stood, wobbled painfully to the trailer door, opened it, and pissed into the gravel. I took in Matt's view. I liked coming here. Matt lived in squalor but our visits were clean. He never asked questions. It didn't matter if it was six months or a year in-between, he always acted like I'd never left.

It's been nine months this time. Except that Matt's missing, nothing else has changed. Rockies to the west. A pumpjack pawing the ground to the east. Close by, the well house and dripping tap, rotting outhouse, cobwebbed shed for rusted tools. Out further, the vomit-green swamp that glows in the twilight and Matt's quarter section of scrub brush.

I stumbled into the sticky July heat, squinted into the naked sky and wished for a baseball cap. I thought I could hear the oil-sucking sounds of the pumpjack, the thump, grind, hum, but it was all in my head. It was Farley's truck I heard. He eased down the gravel and stopped in front of me. Farley has the section of land beside Matt's. Three years ago he gave up on potatoes, planted hay, and pounded in row after row of fence line. His number one job these days is grazing rotation, trundling his bison and elk herds from one square to the next.

Farley's stubby legs hit the dust. "How are you, Jake?" He ambled towards me like I was his best friend. I braced myself as he grabbed my hand, sending a jolt clear to my ear. "Saw car lights. Last night, late. Thought you might be back."

Farley looked me over. My four days of stubble and a neck as shiny and dark as an eggplant. "Not much of a homecoming," he added. "Your brother gone and all."

"Where's he got to?" I asked.

"Well, you read the note, didn't you? Your guess as good as any."

"Matt left a note?"

"Been gone — well, let's see — going on six months now. He took the old truck. Saw him off myself."

"Matt left a note?" I couldn't find anything to lean against.

"I've been out here a dozen times at least." Farley, the good country neighbour. "Just checking. In case he came back."

"Chrissakes, Farley, Matt left a note?"

Farley wrinkled his fat cheeks and rubbed his finger up and down the length of his nose. "Thought you'd a read it by now. Plain as day. On the cot right where I left it."

It was a long way back to the trailer. "Must have missed it. Give me the gist."

"Matt says the place is yours, land and all. The deed's there, too. Says he's not coming back. Says you can burn the trailer like you talked about."

"That it?" I was so dizzy I tilted into him. Farley hopped forward to take my weight, and I shifted my feet to get straight.

"That's it. Make sense to you?"

Farley would like nothing more than to sit across from me and gossip about Matt's peculiarities and this quarter section in need of a master. "Thanks for dropping by, Farley," I said, guiding his shoulder towards his truck door.

"Well, yeah, sure. Let you get settled." Farley hoisted his miniature frame behind the big wheel. "What happened to you anyway? Fall off a rig or something?" He actually winked he was so pleased with his joke.

I winked back and slammed his door with my one good arm, waving him away.

* * *

The company-sponsored doctor ran some tests. It took thirty minutes to drive to the office in Calgary, another fifteen to find a place to park. X-rays, range of motion stuff. Poking and prodding. I shuffled from one green-walled room to the next, filling in forms. I pissed in a cup and watched the blood lady fill six vials. Another lady made me take off my shoes and stand on a scale, then she pointed to a room and ordered me to strip down to my socks.

Williamson, the doctor in charge of my file, knocked on the door.

"Your system has had quite a shock," she said after considerable manhandling.

"When can I go back to work?"

"Kenya, wasn't it?" She rummaged through her papers. "Your ribs will take eight more weeks. Your left arm — we'll wait and see."

"Eight weeks. Jesus."

"That's right. We'll start you on physio. See how you do."

"What am I supposed to do if I can't work?"

Williamson looked up from the file, pushed her glasses up her nose, smiling. "Rest, relax, heal. Take Tylenol 3." She wrote out a prescription. "Your insurance will cover your expenses. Consider it an extended paid leave."

I bought the Tylenol at Shoppers Drug Mart. A herd of giggling girls blocked the magazine aisle, making it difficult to sidestep them. At the counter, I fumbled with the child-proof lid until I finally asked Cindy the Pharmacist to open the bottle. She gave me that "sorry for you" expression, and I popped two, then one more, in front of her. She looked kind of frightened, like she just helped a child swallow rat poison.

"Maximum of two, sir, every four hours."

"Sorry. I didn't bring my glasses. I'll be sure to read all about it when I get back home."

I hobbled back to the truck, my shoulder throbbing — bong, bong, bong. I stopped for a case of beer before I hit the old highway and headed in the direction of Matt's trailer. There's a campground along the river where we go fishing sometimes, about thirty kilometres east of Matt's land. It has five ramshackle sites with picnic tables, firepits and flat patches for tents. One self-pay station, seven bucks a night. One outhouse, one bear-proof garbage bin, one water pump, and the river. Nobody goes there. At the unmarked fork, the pavement turns to gravel, and I slowed down to a crawl to prevent my insides from falling out. Dust filled the cab as the road wound and dipped towards the river, clumps of rock and dried mud heaped high along both sides.

I knew my arm was no good for fishing even if I had my rod, but the beer was cold and I'd have the place to myself. Except I rounded the corner marking the end of the road and there was an old van parked badly in the middle tent spot, like it had run out of gas and coughed to a halt. I memorized the license plate number. This is something I do — memorize license plate numbers. I guess I got shamed into it after that fiasco as a witness. The cops kept saying, can't you remember anything, like the colour of the car or how many men inside? I was just a little kid standing in the wrong place at the wrong time, but it stuck with me, that dummy feeling.

Whoever owned the van had been there awhile. An orange tarp stretched from tree to tree, making a roof for the picnic table. The table was covered with a bright blue tablecloth, plus several boxes, plastic containers, water jugs, and books lined up one side. A bouquet of wild flowers sat in a water-filled jar beside candles stuck onto tinfoil clumps. Large pillows, stacked on the grass; chairs and TV tables arranged around the fire pit like a pretend home. There were girl things strung along a rope tied between two trees: panties, bathing suit tops, thin white socks. No signs of fishing gear. No tent. No people. But shoes lined up on a mat outside the back van door.

I saw all this before I got out of the truck. This had been my fishing hole, mine and Matt's, for as long as I could remember. Now it had squatters, probably pot-soaked tax dodgers who couldn't tell a whitefish from a rainbow. I cut the engine, opened a beer and drained it. I wanted the satisfaction of meeting them.

The truck heated like a furnace under the muggy sky and when the squatters still didn't show, I cracked a second beer, eased myself down to the ground and limped along the riverbank. The river was low, a trickle of its usual self. A person could easily cross from one bank to the other on the giant pink stones. It must have been an unusually dry winter. The hills to the west looked brown and patchy and the dull silver leaves of the willows had curled into themselves, like they'd given up on rain for the season. I could have called Matt while I was gone, chatted about the weather, asked how he was doing. He always talked Mexico. Maybe he was decked out on a beach somewhere in his undershirt and shorts, a tequila bottle propped in sand near his feet, skinny white thighs baking brown.

I could hear their voices long before I saw them, cheerful birdlike chatter blending in with the forest noises and echoing off the water. I found a solid tree stump near some small spruce and sat and waited. Two girls waded through the river. The one in front was in tight blue jean shorts and a tank top, long hair streaked with golds and reds, like Christmas ribbon. A younger girl followed her, a springy little thing in a floppy blue hat and rolled-up overalls, a sandal sticking out from each pocket. She carried a walking stick. I thought they'd wade right by without noticing, but the taller one saw me on my stump.

"Hello," she said. She looked fearless. Like she'd been expecting me all along. I knew that look. A person had to have been through a whole lot of crap to stand before a stranger that way.

She waded towards me, came right over.

"Hello." I stood, requiring several separate movements to get myself upright while managing to hang onto my beer.

"You all right?" She was out of the water by then, hardly pausing as her bare feet slipped along the jagged rocks. The young girl pulled her sandals from her pockets, bent down to put them on, then picked up her stick and followed closely, floppy hat down. The first one looked older than she did from a distance, more sturdy, like she could climb a mountain and not lose her breath. This must be mother and daughter.

"I see you've found my spot." I moved away from my stump towards her.

"I was about to say the same to you." She smiled wide. Her whole face transformed into a child's, her hair like amber glass.

"I've been fishing the spot for years. Never met anyone here until now."

"And you're our first tourist. We've walked up and down this river. Haven't seen any fish."

The young girl poked her head from around her mother, folded back her hat and looked straight at me. She had a pretty face with almond-shaped, frightened eyes. They were full of questions. The kid had more sense than her mother; I knew her look, too. What were they doing out here in the middle of nowhere? I gave the kid my best smile, but she didn't look convinced, hugging her stick closely and leaning into her mother.

We walked towards their campsite, me trying to keep up. The woman looked back every ten paces or so, obviously tracking me.

"Have a seat," she said and pointed to a chair near the fire pit. "You look like you should rest for a minute before you leave." She walked over to the picnic table and straddled her long legs across the bench. The young girl went over to the other side and sat across from her mother.

I sat. "Name's Jake," I offered.

"I'm Harmony and this is Rebee," the mother said.

"Hello, Rebee. You like fishing?"

The girl shrugged without looking up. I wanted her to take off her hat so I could see her face.

"Odd choice for a vacation spot," I said. "Just the two of you?"

"I'd say it's perfect. Up until now, we've had the place to ourselves. Rebee, make some sandwiches, will you, hon. I'll make us some juice."

Harmony poured some crystals into a white plastic jug, then stood up again, leaving her daughter alone with me as she headed towards the water pump at the mouth of the campground, about 100 yards away. I watched her go as Rebee rooted through one of the boxes and pulled out a jar of peanut butter and a package of crackers.

"Looks like you've settled in pretty good. You and your mom been here long?"

Rebee spread thick chunks of peanut butter across a straight row of graham crackers lined on a paper towel. Under the orange tarp roof, her skin was the colour of a grapefruit. She glanced over at her retreating mother, and I figured she'd stay silent, but then she slipped off her hat, looked straight at me, and said, “A couple of weeks, I guess.”

She didn’t correct me about the woman being her mother.

“What you been doing here?”

She shrugged again as though she couldn’t remember. I thought about the gang of giggling girls at the Shoppers that morning, probably at the outdoor pool by now, lying on towels, trying to catch the lifeguard’s eye.

“We go berry-picking.” She licked the knife. “For saskatoons and raspberries. Or read books. Build fires.”

“Rebee your real name?”

“Yes.”

“How old are you, Rebee?”

“Eleven. No-twelve. I had my birthday last week.”

“Twelve. Really? I would have thought you were thirteen at least.”

It was a good thing to say. She smiled, a brief dimpling of her cheeks, then back to her wary look. I left my chair and shuffled over to the shade of the picnic table. Rebee had peanut butter on her cheek. She looked like she could use a bath.

“Were you in a fight?” she asks.

“Nope. An accident.”

“A car accident?”

“Fell off a rig. Bounced down two tiers right into the dirt. Pretty dumb, eh? Can’t work for awhile. Supposed to heal quietly while the doctors check my pulse. Mostly I think they’re afraid of a lawsuit. They’ve told me to stay here and rest.”

“You mean stay *here?*” She’s looked around, frightened, as though this space would crumble under the weight of us all.

“No, no, not here. In Canada. What do you figure I should do now that I can’t work?”

Harmony walked back to us and placed the jug on the table. It was filled with frothy purple juice. Rebee stacked the slathered crackers three at a time and put them on a plastic plate.

"Rebee, you've got peanut butter all over your face."

Rebee glanced at me quickly, wiping her cheek with the back of her hand to smear the brown muck away.

"Want some lunch before you leave?" Harmony said, referring I guess to the cracker sandwiches. She sat down beside me at the table, pulled her hair into a ponytail and tied it with a piece of thin leather, then poured juice into a plastic cup for Rebee, who gulped it down in one long swig.

Only a thief would take food from that table.

"I've got beer in the truck."

"Rebee, be a doll and go get the beer. Don't drop it."

Rebee slid off the bench and went over to the truck. She struggled with the heavy cab door and came back, arms circling the case like a baby. Harmony pulled three from the box, popped off their tops, and handed one to Rebee and me. The kid took it without even blinking.

"I'm looking for my brother. Thought he might have shown up here."

"Not since we've been around. Unless he's a tight-assed warden with nothing better to do than harass campers. I told him, for seven bucks a night, we should at least get toilet paper."

Harmony lazily swatted at the flies crawling over the cracker plate. She examined me like a doctor, with eyes the colour of a Kenyan butter tree. She wore no makeup and the sun had freckled her nose and cheeks.

"Cracked ribs?"

"For a start."

"He fell off a rig into the dirt," Rebee piped up.

Harmony looked hard at the girl, who blushed deep under her mother's stare. Something dark passed between them and Rebee quit talking, just sipped on her beer and chipped away with her thumb at the table's peeling paint. Her index finger bent at the tip like it was dislocated. I tried not to stare.

"My brother's an older guy. Name's Matt. Harmless. He'd have his fishing pole."

"Haven't seen him. Kinda hard to lose a brother, isn't it?"

"Apparently not."

"Maybe he doesn't want to be found."

Something about the way she said this, so matter-of-factly, made me catch my breath. If she knew she was being hurtful, she didn't let on. She was taking her crackers apart, eating one at a time.

"Well, if your brother pops by, I'll tell him you're looking."

I wondered who she was running from to end up here.

I had no view from that table. Tucked into the valley, I couldn't see the wheat fields. Couldn't see the sky. Even the pumpjack in my head had gone silent. I'd had enough of that place.

"Gotta be off, I guess."

Harmony nodded her approval as I stepped away from the table.

"Nice meeting you," I said. "Enjoy the rest of your holiday."

Rebee looked up at me, like she might say something, but didn't. I gritted my teeth to stop from staggering in front of these girls — the pain in my shoulder nearly toppling me — and counted the careful steps, nineteen, eighteen, seventeen, back to the truck. Rebee must have followed, because as I started the engine and was about to back up, she stood at my window, holding the beer case in her arms.

"Harmony wants to know, do you want your beer?"

"Na. You keep it."

She put the case down in the dirt and hung her arms at her sides, her finger crooked as all get out. She caught me staring at her hand and shoved it in her pocket.

"Dollhouses."

"Sorry?"

She glanced back once at her mother, then looked straight at me. "You asked me what you could do now you can't work. Maybe you could start building dollhouses. I read about a guy who did that. In the laundromat."

"A guy built dollhouses in a laundromat?"

"No," Rebee blushed deeply, like she'd made a stupid mistake. "That's just where I read about it. In a newspaper. In a laundromat."

"Right. Good idea. I'll keep that in mind, Rebee."

I nodded reassuringly as I inched the truck backwards. This kid needed homemade chicken noodle soup in the worst way.

* * *

Between trips to the physio office, I've been airing out Matt's trailer, leaving the windows open, propping the door with his hunting rifle. He's squatted over this same patch of scrub grass for two decades now. For all that time, there's little of Matt in here. Two cots at one end. A table, bench and two chairs at the other. In the middle, cupboards and a sink too small to dunk a pot. Matt never hooked up the water anyway. Most days, he'd plunge his head under the pumphouse tap. Once a week, he'd head over to the pool, pay his four dollars, and sit naked in the steam room for an hour at a time. Then he'd shower and shave and take his wrinkled pink skin back to the trailer. During his snowed-in months, he kept from freezing with a propane heater. That and his bourbon.

Across from the sink there's a small closet and a bank of drawers. I shoved what was left of him — four shirts, an old coat, two pairs of grey holey socks, a couple of undershirts and a pair of long underwear — into a garbage bag. Then I took the two drawers outside, one at a time, and weakly pounded the backs of them, scattering curled spiders. From the second drawer, a yellowed photo floated to the ground. I eased myself down and back up again; blew off the dust. A younger, clear-eyed Matt stood beside a woman, his arm around her shoulders, a grin taking over his face. He was shirtless, tall and lean. The woman wore a fancy dress, heeled shoes and patterned stockings. I couldn't think where this picture would be taken. Couldn't imagine my brother finding a day like this.

Matt never cared for women, as far as I knew. Rita was no exception. I brought her to the trailer a few days after the Justice of the Peace ceremony. I wanted the three of us to drive over to the diner, sit like a family. Rita smiled, all teeth, and held out her hand. Matt just threw his fists into his pockets and stared her up and down. Legs, belly, breasts, belly.

"So you got her knocked up," he barked, dismissing Rita and glaring at me. Rita smoothed her dress in front and then clung to my arm.

"Nice," I said. "This is my wife."

We never got to the diner. Rita cried all the way back to our apartment and spread like dough on the bed. I tried to sit beside her but she flung out her arm, pushed me away and hissed, "What kind a family you come from? What you got me into?"

I never liked Rita much. All those large teeth crowded into a small mouth and a duck voice that made people look in her direction every time she got going. When she told me she was pregnant, I was dumbstruck, couldn't believe all that heaving and thrusting in her father's house had led to a baby. We were hardly more than kids ourselves. Married only six weeks when she confessed, tears raining down her watermelon belly, the baby wasn't mine, for sure it wasn't, but Big Barry Chugg's, the guy before me. She said she and Barry had been on the outs and she was scared of what her father would do if nobody came to claim her. Big Barry and Rita patched up their differences while I worked the night shift at the sawmill. I hugged her tightly when she asked for the divorce papers. I was so relieved at this second chance I got back-to-back speeding tickets on my way to the lawyer's.

After Rita left with Big Barry, I started checking on Matt again. He never did apologize, acted like Rita and the baby never were.

"You should have treated her with more respect," I said one night in front of the fire.

"Yah, that would've been better." He beat the flames with the metal poker. "I sometimes don't think."

"I was trying to do right."

"What — by marrying her?"

"That's right."

"You try too hard, Jake," he said in a gentle scolding voice.

"Whadda you know about right and wrong?

"What do you know about it?" I shot back.

"Whad I know? I know that 'right' can sit on the butt end of feeling good. Sometimes you gotta turn a situation upside down to figure it out. That girl wasn't yours. Never was. You'd a made her miserable, and she you, and then all your righteousness wouldn't be worth a damn."

There was a sadness in his voice, a longing almost. I got the feeling his words were for him, not me and Rita; that he was remembering why he'd chosen a godforsaken trailer in the middle of scrub over a life with commitments and improvements and plodding forward.

Back in the trailer, I propped the photo against the Scotch, then I dragged Matt's mattress, blankets, and shirts into the back of the truck, and out to the dump, paid my $4.50, and heaved them over the cliff and into the smoking heap. When I got back, drenched in sweat, I found the brace and Velcroed it to my arm, poured myself a tumbler, washed down three Tylenols and waited for the shakes to subside. I studied the photo, the light on their faces. I wanted to reach in and pull out the answers to my questions. Things I should have asked him. All his doing without. All his doing nothing to change.

He should have asked, too. I'd worked the rigs for two decades, in countries so cold you were scared to take a piss, so hot you could lick up the salt pouring out of you. Bad equipment, bad conditions. Such lousy food I'd dream about Safeway — about sprawling on top of the lettuce display. In all that time, he never asked about any of it.

Maybe falling off a rig is a wake-up call. Matt's leaving, too. I wanted to think I was a part of his plan, even if I was only on the butt end of feeling good.

* * *

I musta looked pretty bad. The kid wearing the grocery store apron kept five feet between us and kept glancing at me sideways as he carried the bags to the truck. I got beer, wine, an assortment of pops, ice, three steaks, potatoes, corn on the cob, butter, a bumbleberry pie, toilet paper, a teen magazine and a giant roll of tinfoil.

I rounded the corner a few minutes before four, groceries rattling on the seat beside me, dust trailing behind. When I spotted the van and the girls stretched out on those big pillows reading their books, I felt the muscles in my neck relax. I had no business going back. But after a week in the trailer with Matt's ghost, I told myself I needed company; lightness and laughter and girl talk. I didn't know if it was Harmony or Rebee I needed to see.

All I knew was something had been rankling me ever since I found them. Their playing house beside a dried-up river, with their make-believe lunch of peanut butter and purple Kool-Aid, their rundown van, their washing hung like rags on a ratty rope, a whisper of trouble between them.

Rebee jumped up right away. Harmony just leaned on her arm and stared. "Brought you some toilet paper," I yelled to her as I stepped out of the truck. My shoulder throbbed mercilessly, a burning beat, like it housed its own heart. Rebee was beside me. I touched her shoulder, smiled and handed her the two lightest bags.

"Sorry, wasted trip," Harmony said. "Your brother hasn't shown if that's what you're after. And we got to the store yesterday."

"Yeah, but I bet you didn't think of a bumbleberry pie."

"I've forgotten your name."

I looked at her closely for evidence of a lie, but couldn't find anything in her blank expression.

"Jake. Melanie and Phoebe, right?"

Harmony stood, stretching long brown arms over her head, hands clasped, flexing the muscles of her striking legs. She wore a black two-piece bathing suit and a beaded ankle bracelet. I tried not to gawk. When Rebee and I got to the table and started unloading the groceries, Harmony wrapped a coloured skirt around her hips and came over to join us.

"Thought we could share a couple of steaks."

Rebee was in her same overalls as last time, her nose in one of the bags, her throat circled in a necklace of grime.

"Did you? You in the habit of inviting yourself into someone's space? I've met people like you."

"Like me? I don't think so. But technically, this is my space. I found it first. And I come bearing gifts."

I pulled out the teen magazine and passed it to Rebee.

"I'm not sure this is the kind you like." Rebee smiled and nodded. I decided I liked making her smile.

Harmony sat on the picnic bench and looked over the goods. "Why do people keep wanting to feed us? I could tell you we have plans."

"I'd figure it out. I'd build a fire at spot number four and cook my steaks, and wave at you every so often, and then I'd notice you weren't going anywhere, so I'd figure your plans fell through and I'd invite you over for supper, and you'd ask, 'Anything I can bring?' and I'll say, all the dishes, a couple of chairs, and the tablecloth, please."

Rebee giggled into her hand and Harmony looked faintly

amused. I decided I could stay. We settled into the preparations with hardly a word. We threw the ice in the banged-up cooler, and scattered the pop cans and beer in the empty spaces, of which there were plenty. Rebee chose a ginger ale and I opened two beers and passed one to Harmony. She sent Rebee into the forest to gather kindling and I built the fire high at first, then let it mellow to hot red coals. Rebee and I scrubbed the potatoes in the river. Then we lathered them with butter, wrapped them in tinfoil and threw them on the coals beside the corn.

Rebee moved her pillow to the shade of the van. She lay on her stomach, feet in the air, thumbing through her magazine. Harmony and I sat under the tarp on opposite sides of the table.

"So how long you going to be here?" I asked.

"No idea," Harmony said. Rebee looked up from her magazine and focused on her mother's back with a troubled stare.

"Do you live around here?"

"No."

"But we lived in Coaldale for awhile," Rebee called over. "Coaldale's close isn't it?"

"Not too close," I answered. "We're closer to Calgary."

"We lived in Calgary, too," Rebee said.

"Who's talking to you, Rebee," Harmony said, not turning around.

"Sounds like you've lived in a lot of places," I called back, taken off guard by Harmony's stony expression.

Rebee just nodded.

"Me, too," I said. I thought of pumpjacks. Of places blurred into one long row of makeshift metal bunks and variegated siding, airplane sinks, the snores of many men, brown, black, and yellow. Of Matt and the trailer I called home.

Harmony cracked two more beers and handed one to me. When she brought out a deck of cards, Rebee bounced over and sat beside me. We chose 21, taking turns winning, using pinecones for chips. Rebee played like she'd shuffled a thousand decks. Not a weary practice. Not like on the rigs, all our dealing cards as a way to shift time, bored to madness, itching for a fight, for something, anything.

Rebee just seemed easy is all. Her mother, too. They slapped cards on the table, locking eyes every so often like they shared a language that required no words. We avoided conversation that could lead to anything, stuck to card talk instead. Harmony didn't ask what I was looking for and I didn't ask her. Those questions just hung in the air beneath the tarp.

For dinner, Harmony lit candles inside plastic cups and placed one beside each of our plates while I opened the wine. Harmony picked at her food. Rebee gobbled down her man-sized steak and two fat pieces of pie, berry juice dribbling from the corner of her mouth. I thought I could see her belly expand, like a snake that had swallowed an egg, and I considered it an accomplishment, to fill her up like that.

Before Rebee went into the van, sleepy from excess, she gave me a necklace of rosehips, strung together with thick black thread. For good luck she said. Harmony walked me to the truck and closed the door softly behind me. The air had turned frosty and she was wrapped in a striped blanket.

"Goodbye, Jake." Her fingertips rested on my open window.

"You take care now," I replied. I wanted to tell her I'd see her again.

Driving home in the dark, I remembered my broken left side for the first time in five hours. I swallowed three Tylenol with a swig of lukewarm beer and slowed to a crawl on the empty black road. Rebee's rosehips dangled from my mirror. I thought about pumpjacks in open fields and riches rising from deep below the dirt.

* * *

Rita taught me one thing: don't get caught without money. Even back then, all crackling and boyish green, I knew something was off-kilter. There I was, lashed to a girl I could barely stand, and all I could think of was money. I didn't think about a lifetime of getting liquored up so I could bear to wake beside her, of gritting my teeth and steeling myself for a storm every time I walked through the door, of closing my eyes and pretending she was someone else, and I was a different man, and we were two people easy with each other. I didn't think about any of that. All I could focus on was not being poor.

I've enough to haul away Matt's trailer and replace it with a manor. To buy out Farley and ship his herds north. Or to hire the detective with the flashiest ad.

He charges $500 a day, plus expenses. Elroy Lloyd is his name. For all his ad's sizzle, he looked less than dangerous. He was tall and skinny and wearing a ridiculous pink shirt buttoned tight at the neck. I imagined him being trampled at the supermarket when the dollar daze announcement came over the loudspeaker.

"You any good?" I asked. We had this conversation in his small Calgary office on the second floor of the professional building.

"I'll get the job done," he said. "Although I won't guarantee the results will be what you're hoping for."

I had no recent pictures of Matt. None, in fact, except the one of him with the woman taken back twenty years or more. I wasn't about to hand this to Elroy.

He asked about family, friends, enemies. Business partners. Women. A wife? Partner? Lover, maybe?

His questions gave me a worse headache. I just wanted to find my brother, not dissect his inadequacies.

I gave Elroy a fat wad of cash and he told me to check in at least twice a week. With no place else to go, I went back to the trailer. Hauled out the shed junk and stacked the rotted wood and garbage near the fire pit. Fixed the latch on the outhouse door, poured processed lime down the hole, swept webs off the corners and ceiling, reminded myself to buy toilet paper.

I thought about my day with Harmony and Rebee. About Rebee forgetting to hide her finger's crookedness while she clutched her cards. How when she laughed, tilting her head back, she could have been a desert flower sucking up water in a flash of rain. The way Harmony's hair brushed against my shoulder as I passed her the plates to wash in the river. Her smell of earth and sun. The way the firelight caught her eyes before she melted into the dark. I imagined Matt's land, my land now, with a two-storey house. A picture window and yellow marigolds in pots. Harmony, Rebee, Matt and me on white deck chairs, drinking iced tea, staring east, away from the pumpjack.

I thought about the men in this world who settle next to the rhythm of a woman, one woman, their whole lives. That one guy coming off a middle-of-the-night flight after a seven-weeks-on, three-off rotation. He practically leaped into the aisle when the plane finally docked and the lights came up. He jogged past our dog-tired group, smiled at the customs officer, and bypassed the escalator, taking four steps at a time. The waiting room was crammed like always. But he found her in an instant, home in her arms.

I'm a believer. I just don't know how it's done is all. What kind of chromosomes, hormones, cyclones bring all that together? Do you fall hard for a woman because of the light in her hair? The look she gets when she's looking at you? And if you fall for one reason, do you stay for another, until there comes a time when you can't remember why you fell in the first place but you don't even notice because it no longer matters. Somewhere between your falling and landing, what floats in between? What anchor drops to hold a man steady?

I was at the sink, patching the hose, when Farley showed, eyes barely clearing his wheel. He had a pair of antlers tied to his hood. He stepped out of his truck and I stepped out of the trailer, crunching through gravel until we met in the middle. Grinning, he handed me a basket tied with a green ribbon. "The Mrs. wanted you to have some muffins. Orange bran with raisins." He seemed especially pleased.

I looked down at him and caught the glint of the silver buffalo head cinching up his pants.

"Your brother was a good man, Jake," he started. "You're a lot like him, you know."

"You talk like he's dead."

"I don't think that. Just don't think we'll be seeing him anymore, that's all."

"Thanks for stopping by."

"Least I could do." He stood his ground, as though the conversation was not over. I figured if I went back into the trailer I'd find him at my table.

"Wha'd you want, Farley?" He blushed. I moved in close to block him from coming further.

"Want to know how you're getting along."

"And what I'm going to do with this quarter section?"

"Well, that too, I suppose. I'll give you a fair price. No question about that."

"I appreciate your concern, but go home, okay? I'll let you know when I'm ready to talk."

Farley blushed deep, turned on his heel, and left without another word. I finished patching the hose at the trailer sink. After the taps quit spewing and the water ran clear, I built a fire with the last of the shed wood and roasted hot dogs, eating them off the stick. An African sky, breezeless, mosquito gauze layers above the smoke. I could hear Farley's bull elk in the distance, bawling like their hearts were broken. I thought I could hear the thump, grind, and hum of the pumpjack too.

* * *

A ridiculous August evening, even by Alberta standards. Fat flakes crisscrossed my windshield in the driving wind like a field of white daisies. Despite my low beams, the road was hard to follow. The heater blasted stinky heat. Campers from Okotoks to Pincher Creek would be layering up, hunkering down in the bottom of their bags or packing for home. I'd stuffed a duffel bag with all I could find: two wool blankets, a couple of sweaters, an old fleece jacket, and one pair of thermal mittens. I stopped at the Dairy Queen and asked Lisa the Hostess to fill my thermos with hot chocolate. She didn't know how to ring up a thermos, so I ordered two extra larges, filled it myself and saved both paper cups.

The local radio station guy compared this to a night back in 1922, recorded in history's weather books as the storm of the century. He gave us "Frosty the Snowman" sung by a choir of kids. I fiddled with the buttons and almost missed the campground turn. The truck slipped sideways down the incline. I shifted into neutral, eased my foot on the brake, and skated to a stop several feet from the van. I kept the lights on and the truck running and stepped down into six inches of slushy muck.

No girls in sight. By the looks of things, they didn't try too hard to find shelter for their stuff. Pillows lay buried on the white ground, towels twisted into sopping lumps hung on tree branches. The orange tarp nearly touched the tabletop, sagging deeply under the heavy snow.

"Helloooo. It's Jake."

I said this just loud enough so they'd hear my voice over my truck's noisy idle. I thought they must be huddled in the van, and I wanted them to know it was only me. I wanted them to hope it was me; that they'd been counting on it.

"Helloooo. It's Harmony."

I jerked my head backward, causing such pain down my left side it actually heated my fingertips. She'd come up from behind me on the riverside, not helpless at all.

"Sorry. Didn't mean to startle you." She was wrapped in her striped blanket, a halo of snowflakes on top of her head, white chunks clinging to her eyelashes. Her breath formed wispy puffs in the air between us.

"No, no, that's all right." I tried to get my breath back by counting silently through the pain. "Thought you were in the van."

"Rebee's inside. I was going stir crazy. Came out to look for the moon."

It was nearly a whiteout. No moon up there.

"Brought you some blankets and stuff. Hot chocolate for Rebee."

"You're a regular Santa Claus. Want to walk with me?"

She was in sandals, bare toes. No coat under that blanket I'd bet. She was not breathing bourbon, so I couldn't guess what stopped her from freezing. I looked past her to her tracks coming up from the river. She'd left a deep wet puddle with each step, like miniature swimming pools.

"Harmony, on my scale for worst walking weather, this is a nine. If it starts to hail golf balls, I'll bump it to ten. There's Scotch in the truck. Want to sit in the cab and warm up?"

"I'm not cold." She shook her head to remove some of the snow. She was not exactly needy. "But I'll go for the Scotch."

She slogged her way to the other side of the truck. I looked over to the van for signs of Rebee, didn't find any, so we got in the truck and I threw the stuff I'd brought into the back seat, the thermos under my seat.

"It's like a sauna in here," she said, closing the door quietly.

I opened the window a crack and turned down the heat, then passed her the bottle. She closed her eyes and took a long swig.

I fiddled with the radio, found a station with easy music, and turned the volume way down. The clock read 9:40.

"They say it's a friggin' record. This snow in August. 1922 might have come close."

"Can we take a drive?"

She rubbed her blanket in a circle on her fogged side window, creating a hole to the outside the size of a face. The piling snow pressed down. I turned the wipers on and cleared the front window.

"Sure. I thought maybe you and Rebee might like to get out of here tonight. Stay at a hotel maybe. Wait it out."

"Just a drive would be good." She took a second long swig.

On my scale of worst drive-for-no-reason weather, this got a ten. She probably had no money. "I can pick up the room tab. Maybe we can get something to eat before I drop you girls off."

She stared straight ahead, as though we were already on the road and her view kept changing.

"No strings," I said. She didn't reply. I was not going to push it. "Okay. Want me to get Rebee? I brought her some hot chocolate."

"You said that already. We'll leave her in the van."

She must have known I was staring at her, but she wouldn't look at me. I knew nothing about kids, but I did remember those winter nights where the adults got lost and you couldn't find them anywhere. I didn't want to leave Rebee alone in the van.

"She'll be fine, Jake. She's sleeping," Harmony said without turning to face me.

"But what if she wakes and finds you gone? What if she's cold?"

"You worry about all the wrong stuff. Want to go for a drive or not?"

I turned the wipers to high and checked the van once more. The west wind was driving the snow at a sharp angle, leaving the back van window clear. No sign of her.

I backed away slowly, sliding in the slush, having a hard time getting the truck turned around, a harder time still getting up the steep incline to the main road.

"Which way?"

"Just away."

I turned right, the direction I just came from. There was no one else on the two-lane road so I drove down the centre. We didn't speak for several kilometres, just stared through the ribbon of white my headlights made, taking turns with the bottle. Harmony's blanket crumpled around her like a Kleenex, her hair plastered to her forehead, clinging to her sweater. She took her sandals off and placed them on top of the dash vent. I turned up the heat again.

"I hired a detective."

"A detective? For what?"

"To find my brother."

"Really?"

"Yep. Elroy PI."

"What will you do if you find him?"

"Don't know. Haven't got that far."

"You must care about him a lot, to go to all that bother."

"Kinda dumb, eh? When I was in Kenya this last time, nine months almost, I didn't think about him once. Now that he's gone, I can't stop."

I'd been thinking about what a sorry brother I've made, but I didn't say this out loud. I'd been thinking, too, about the lives of Harmony and Rebee and wondered just then if the kid had bad dreams. I thought to myself how much thinking a person gets into when he can't work. "How about you?" I asked her. "Anybody out looking for you?"

"Oh, I doubt that. Was he a good brother?"

"Not particularly. No brothers, uncles, fathers of your own? Husband, maybe?"

"Why is it that when a man wants to find out about a woman, he asks about her men?"

Why was it she wouldn't answer even one question?

She turned her body, leaning against her door, and stretched her legs so her feet rested on my lap. Her toes were tinged with blue and I covered them with my hand. She was smiling at me, lip slightly curled. I tried to keep my eyes on the road.

"Maybe you just can't stand the fact that he didn't say goodbye," she said.

Maybe. Maybe I was just mad he ended what we had without my say. It was hard to concentrate with this woman laid out before me.

We passed a car in the ditch, angled sideways, back end sticking up, and I slowed down and inched alongside, checking for bodies. Harmony ignored the vehicle, didn't feign the slightest interest, and when I saw it was empty, we picked up speed again and kept going.

"You live around here, right? Or your brother does. Can I see your place?"

When we drove through the gate she looked from the sludge-filled swamp to the outhouse to the sagging trailer. Since Rita, I hadn't brought another woman here. The place almost looked decent in its blanket of white. It had nearly stopped snowing, just leftover circles of flakes, the air so clear and new it sparkled. Harmony didn't say a word. Before I was even out of the cab, she headed to the trailer. By the time I got inside, she was leaning against the sink, looking out the small window.

"Home sweet home," I said loudly. The power was out again. I lit the candle from the knife drawer and put it on the table. "Just spin around once and you'll have had the grand tour. Not much, I know. Now you've seen it, wanna go?"

"We just got here. I need a drink." She smiled.

I went and got the bottle from the truck. When I got back, she was sitting at the table, wrapped in her blanket. I rummaged through the cupboard, found two glasses and poured us each a drink.

"Is this Matt?" She reached for the yellowed picture and held it against the flickering candle.

I nodded.

"Who is the woman?"

"Don't know. Found the picture in his drawer."

"She's radiant."

"Matt liked to pay for his women. Pay 'em and leave 'em."

"Not with this woman. Look at her. Look at your brother with her."

She handed me the picture and I studied him closely again. This picture looked nothing like Matt, though it reminded me of the man I saw him to be. After my dad left for good, Matt used to come home to visit mother and me. I can't remember my mother's face. White lace-up shoes. A checkered cotton dress. Mostly, it's her voice I remember, husky sounding, like she always had a sore throat. Matt would show up for breakfast on Saturday mornings, sit at his usual spot in our crowded kitchen, and my mother would bring us each two soft-boiled eggs in tiny yellow cups. "Each day your bones need two," she'd tell me in her gravelly voice, as though strong bones were what a boy most needed. Then she'd leave our table and disappear. For hours, for days. Matt never said too much during his visits. Didn't fix stuff or give us money. But he kept coming back, regular as a paycheque, and for that I was grateful. When our mother died, just before Rita showed up, I'd drag my seventeen-year-old weary body to Matt's trailer on Saturday mornings, and he'd feed me soft-boiled eggs.

"You hold onto this, Jake," Harmony said, her finger touching mine as she pointed to the picture in my hand. "Don't let this go."

We drank Scotch in the semi-dark, Matt and his woman taking up the space between us. When Harmony told me she felt cold, I started to stand, to find her a dry blanket, and she stood too, and we bumped into each other in the cramped little space. She was shivering hard and I wrapped me around her as best I could. I wanted her, badly in fact, but I wanted to get it right more. I felt I could do this, whatever it was. This tenderness or softening or cautious unravelling. She buried her face to my neck, held my ribs in place. She smelled like the river, wet earth. My fingers caught in her hair. We pressed against each other until my knees felt weak.

"I need to go home," she said finally, untangling from me, looking up with huge eyes.

I thought she was telling me she needed to go home. Home to her people. To doors that opened for friends and neighbours.

"I'll take you anywhere you want to go. The truck's all

gassed up. We'll have the road to ourselves. We can drive all night."

But she shook her head as though I was confused. "Just get me back to Rebee. She'll be frantic."

I instantly felt my stomach roll. "Of course we'll get Rebee. You said she'd be sleeping."

"She doesn't sleep for shit, Jake." Her voice had hardened again, those traces of softness all gone. "Just put me back where you found me, okay?"

We drove slowly back to the campground, plowing through the sludge. Harmony sat on her side of the cab, me on mine.

"Can you find my place again, now that you've been there? It's twenty-seven kilometres from the campground to the trailer."

She didn't answer me, so I repeated, "Twenty-seven kilometres due east. You can clock it on your odometer."

"I'm a good mother," she whispered.

I pulled her towards me and wrapped one arm around her and she curled into my shoulder. We didn't speak again. When I slid the truck to a stop, shadows flickered inside the van, Rebee's candle or lantern, maybe. I wanted to open the door for Harmony, but she got out too fast. We met just as her hand started to turn the rusted handle of the van's back door. I kissed her on the cheek like we were seventeen and her father was waiting on the other side. But it was Rebee who waited. Her almond eyes locked onto mine from behind the frosty window, then disappeared.

I went to the truck and pulled out the thermos, but when I came back to the van, Harmony was already inside. I knocked on the door, and knocked again. Finally, there was nothing left for me to do but go. Rebee's rosehips jumped when I slammed the truck door. They still dangled from my mirror, dark and withered now, like a string of tired eyes. They had that trapped-inside-the-nightmare look, like Rebee. Tonight I was the cause of her bad dreams, but I had the feeling it happened a lot for her. My tires hurled dirty chunks of snow muck as they ground out and away. At the halfway point between the girls' home and mine, I stopped the truck and stepped down, leaving the door open and the engine running. I limped stiffly down the middle of the highway, splashing slop, the hot chocolate thermos pressed to my chest. The pumpjack was out there, anchored to a field, but I couldn't see that far, just the sheepish remains of a blustering storm, the bearded fence lines and toppling white wheat. I marched on, unscrewing the thermos top and pouring slowly. Brown liquid trickled to the ground and melted into a steaming row of *splunks* where the highway's centre line should have been. Then I shook out the last drop and hurled that thermos into the night with everything my good arm would give.

* * *

I woke up already hung over, knotted and fluey. The dream leaked out of me and into the trailer's stillness. It was the dream where I'm a little kid and my father drives me into the backwoods. He parks the truck at the locked gate and we walk along a thistled fence line to the place where the land drops. He lifts me over the barb wire first and then hurdles himself over effortlessly. I follow him straight into the deafening noise until I let his hand slip from mine, cover my ears and stumble and slip, dropping farther and farther behind. He's ahead now, standing at the base of the towering pumpjack. The giant black paw screeches and swoops straight towards him. I think it's going to pluck him from the earth and carry him upwards. Over and over, the angry paw swings. My father waves to come join him but my feet won't move. The pumpjack screams so loud I can't hear his words. In the dream, I turn and run along the endless row of thistles until the noise is just a faint rumble, and my father has disappeared. I wake up each time all prickling and breathless, then I lie in bed and go over that day until I can't stand thinking about it anymore. The way I remember it, I stayed planted near the fence. My father came to me finally and led me by the hand to the truck. He wiped the snot from my nose with a hankie from his pocket. Gave me a stick of gum. Strapped on my seatbelt.

He might have been whistling, but his eyes gave him away. They told how he felt about the sissy boy beside him, afraid of a little oil.

In the trailer, the after-the-storm air tasted wet and smelled like Harmony. I lay on the mattress a long time, staring at the grimy ceiling. I stayed there until I couldn't put it off any longer. I had an appointment with the detective. Farley was in his field, straddling a quad with his stubby legs, surveying the storm's damage the way good farmers do. He waved at me wildly as I drove by.

Today, Elroy PI wore a bright yellow shirt that billowed over his chest and shoulders like a girl's nightie. He sat on the other side of his desk, clucking into the phone while I waited, something about it'll be all right dear and you're better off now it's out in the open. I wondered if the client was imaginary, if I was his only one, and he was whispering soothingly to a dial tone to prepare me for the worst.

"My apologies for that, Jake," he said, slamming the phone down. "Thanks for coming in."

"Have you found him yet?" Elroy PI had sugar sparkles glittering on his chin. No sign of the doughnut box.

"Unfortunately, no. He hasn't turned up."

I waited. Elroy pushed back his chair, stood, and came over to my side of the desk. He hopped up awkwardly and crossed one gangly leg over the other, grabbed onto his bony knee with both hands, leaned back and gave me a sympathetic look. I wanted to shake him until his teeth rattled.

"Don't be disheartened, Jake. There's good news in this. Morgues, hospitals, police stations — all clear. License checks — nothing. Airlines — nothing. I've been very thorough. Your brother doesn't appear to be dead or dying."

"So now what?"

"You mentioned Mexico. Technically speaking, Mexico makes it harder. They just don't have the connections we can hook into from here."

"So what do you suggest?"

"Do you want me to keep going?"

Elroy studied me, his eyes on mine unfaltering, rock steady. He looked like he'd toned it down a notch or two, grown up all of a sudden. I admitted there might be more to the man than his bumblebee outfit. Maybe I'd been itching to slap the sugar from his chin with a rolled up newspaper for all the wrong reasons. Maybe I hadn't been listening. All I know is he was making me decide. Matt was probably not anywhere he didn't want to be. My decision what I wanted to do with that.

"Could you get to Mexico?" I asked.

"I could and I would. It's your decision."

"For $500 a day, of course."

"If we keep going, it's the next logical step."

There was nothing logical here. I handed him another wad of cash. It wasn't hope I was buying, just time.

* * *

Dollhouses are hard to find. I ended up on the outskirts of High River at a converted country house called Charlie's Dollhouse Shop. There was a swinging sign above the creaky summer cottage door with a painting of a two-storey home in the palm of a man's hand. As I entered, an old guy's voice chirped from the back, "Be with you in a minute."

It was a small place, crammed from floor to ceiling with bins of miniatures in baggies. Little porcelain toilets and bathtubs, baby cradles, chairs that rock, candlesticks the size of matches, tea sets no bigger than a child's fingernail. Black Labs with sticks in their mouths, cats curled into circles, mommies, daddies, children of all little sizes. Cows, ducks, pigs. Crabapple trees and evergreens, tiny wicker flower baskets. Charlie had all the fixings.

"And how can I help you today, sir?" He'd come out from behind a set of red curtains. He looked like a dollhouse man, miniature himself, maybe half my height. Stooped shoulders, tiny round wire spectacles, balding head, an old-fashioned red sweater and wool pants with suspenders. I picked up a little porcelain grandpa wrapped in plastic. They could be brothers.

"Are you Charlie?" I dropped the man back to his bin and extended my arm to shake hands.

"The one and only. What can I do you for today?"

We shook hands. “Name’s Jake. Looking for a dollhouse.”

“Come to the right place. Got a model in mind?”

I stared at him blankly.

“Haven’t seen you in here before. New to the dollhouse world?”

I started to laugh when he said this, but he was perfectly serious, so I pretended to clear my throat.

“I’m not really taking it up. I just want a dollhouse. One dollhouse. Like that one over there.” I pointed to the table display in front of the cash register.

“Ah, the Hillsdale. She’s a beauty.”

He instructed me with a wave of his arm to follow him until we stood over the Hillsdale like God and his sidekick. The house was about as big as a beer cooler. Two storeys, blue-painted wood with a multi-gabled roof and a wrap-around white gazebo porch. A solid country home for a farmer and his family.

“Straight out of the heartland and rich in tradition,” Charlie said.

I put my hands behind my back so as not to topple the whole thing over with my clumsy fingers, then I bent down and stuck my eye against the top-storey window. It was the farmer’s bedroom. Gold-etched pictures on the walls, white doilies on the dressers, a full length mirror in a wooden frame.

“One-inch-scale furniture, moving pieces, durable all wood, pre-cut, and easy assembly,” he said.

“I’ll take it. And everything inside too.”

“This is a display model, son,” he said. “They don’t come pre-assembled. You have to build the Hillsdale yourself.”

“I’ll take this one.”

“Sorry, that’s not how it works,” Charlie shuffled behind

the counter. He eyed me up and down, sniffing for danger. I wondered if he had a gun under the shelf. I figured I had to level with him or these negotiations would go sour.

"Charlie, it's for this kid I know. A friend of mine. She just had her twelfth birthday. Name your price."

"Name's Jake, you said?"

I nodded impatiently, wanting to get on with it.

"These houses need to be personally crafted by an adult — sanded, glued, painted. They're one-of-a-kind collectibles. I can sell you the kit. Got two in the back."

"I don't have time to build her this house," I said, reaching into my jeans pocket for my wallet.

"But that's the whole point. It takes time to build one of these."

"She'll be leaving soon. The girl and her mother. It'll be too late." I was embarrassed by the way my words tumbled out.

"These houses are not toys." Charlie took off his glasses and wiped them on a counter rag, then returned them to his face, hooking one ear at a time. His fingers were age-spotted and jittery, and I wondered how they could put together such delicate, tiny pieces. He studied me closely, cheeks crinkling, his eyes magnified behind his glasses, seeing everything. Cracked ribs, swollen joints, bruised heart, the works.

"She's old for her age," I said, my voice barely more than a whisper.

"A lot of love went into this particular Hillsdale."

"Like I said, just name your price."

"You're sure now."

"Absolutely," I replied, though I wasn't sure of anything anymore.

¥ ¥ ¥

Last Monday, the physiotherapists told me I was finished. Our eight weeks were done. I called on Elroy PI and told him he was done too. He put his hand on my shoulder and said I was making the right choice.

Dr. Williamson handed me another prescription for Tylenol 3 this morning. I can breathe without wincing, but my left arm still can't unscrew a jar of pickles.

I must have banged my left side just hard enough for something inside to come unstuck. Somewhere between my falling off a rig and my sitting at this table, I decided. I'm done. I'm done with landscapes not mine, with places where I need a work visa to tell me who I am. I'll get a building permit instead, start with the foundation, and work my way up.

I've got the Hillsdale displayed on the trailer's tabletop. Charlie took his time packaging her up for me. He rummaged behind the curtain for the right-sized box, then he wrapped the furniture and tiny knickknacks in bubbled plastic. He talked the whole time, cautioning me about house moving, location-location-location, the dry Alberta air. As I was leaving, he threw in some landscaping — yellow shrubs and a fuzzy green mat for grass. He asked if I wanted the family to go with it, but I said no. I drove straight from Charlie's to the campground, the Hillsdale strapped beside me on the front seat.

I knew they were gone before I started down the little hill. I could smell their leaving in the empty air. Tidy packers. No wine corks, no bottle caps, no paper trail. No trace at all, aside from the deep grooves of tires spinning through wet ground. I parked in their empty space and sat at their empty picnic table, chipping paint with my thumbnail. Then I walked along the river. A breeze scattered the leaves in the trees, dropping speckled shadows across my path. When I got to where I first spotted them, I chose the whitest bark from the gnarly old birch tree, and carved "Rebee was here" with my army knife. Harmony was never really here; her life was tangled up elsewhere. I knew how that was.

It's a fine-looking house. The architect can scale the plan, add a few more rooms, make it fit this land. From my top-storey room, facing west, I might be able to see the pumpjack with a pair of binoculars. If Matt comes home, the main floor bedroom will save him the stairs.

I could see Farley's truck signalling at my gate. I headed outside to greet him, limping only slightly. I'd offer him a cup of coffee, see what shape his face screwed into over that.

REBEE

WE PULLED IN LAST NIGHT — HARMONY, VIC, AND ME. We slept awful in our stuffy motel room. Normally, Vic only has to stop fidgeting for a few minutes and she's asleep — doesn't matter where she is, sitting on the toilet, leaning against a wall. We shared a bed and every time she rolled towards me I rolled away. My skin felt shivery and my lungs ached and I wanted to open the window but it was nailed shut. Harmony had the other bed to herself. Every time I got up to go to the bathroom she was staring at the ceiling.

Vic smoked up a storm, and when her Players were all gone, she sent me to pick up a pack from the vending machine in the coffee shop. I felt my skin getting crisper, like burning rice paper. It hurt to breathe and a sharp pain drove through my forehead when I moved, like I'd been buried in hot sand upside down with my eyes wide open.

I don't know why I walked past the cigarettes

and sat down in the red booth. I concentrated on the napkin holder, which was almost empty, only two wrinkly blue ones, like somebody had used them and shoved them back in. I stared at the salt and pepper shakers shaped like cows.

"You feeling okay?" The waitress wore nylons under her frilly orange uniform, and when she reached across the booth to put down a cup, the darker brown of the nylon showed at the top of her thick legs.

"You want a menu, hon?"

My hand felt as hot as my head. Smouldering.

"Just a coffee." I clenched the coins for Vic's cigarettes and let them clink to the table. The waitress was back with the coffee pot before I noticed she'd been gone. I almost reached for the cow instead of the sugar. That waitress stood there beside me like a bodyguard, staring at my mallet finger, its floppy pink end. I put that hand under the table and sat on it.

"You let me know if you need anything else," she backed away, but I could feel her stare even though she was gone.

I sipped the awful coffee and thought how nice it would be to disappear. I'd seen it happen once when the Shriners did a show in Calgary and the third-graders got free tickets. When we spilled off the bus, the boys stamped on all the girls' toes while the teacher split us into partners, and we had to hold hands as we marched down the aisle to the right row. I was the extra, two making three, and the girls let go of my hand as soon as our shoes hit the carpet. Girls were oohing and giggling, boys elbowing each other to get to their seats. I inched myself down to the end, to the open space between the front row and the stage. When I looked back, I couldn't spot a single face I recognized. An usher shoved me into an empty seat in the front row just before the lights went down. I sat by a girl with thick glasses. She had the hiccups.

First clowns and jugglers. Then a man in a glittery vest with long tails and a puffy shirt. He stood on the stage pulling fire from air and rabbits from a hat. The halo of light surrounding him surrounded me, too. He was looking right at me. Then he disappeared in a puff of smoke and the auditorium went black, and all the children gasped. It got so quiet the room stopped breathing. A beam of white shot out of the ceiling and landed right on me. I thought for sure God would strike me down even though Harmony says God is nowhere you can find him. I thought I had made him disappear. But then, poof. There he was. In the seat beside me, his face shiny with sweat, eyes twinkling. All the children started clapping; I clapped too, and the man touched my shoulder and then hopped back on the stage and bowed.

The waitress came back with the coffee pot. "You sure you feeling okay, honey?"

She leaned in close. I was afraid she might reach down and touch my head.

I pressed against the plastic.

"I'm real sorry, hon. Hope things get better for you."

"I'm good, thanks." My throat hurt so much I nearly choked.

"Take all the time you need."

I wanted to stay in that booth, close to the waitress who was sorry, and not go back to the sisters who weren't. The coffee tasted terrible. I swallowed a few more mouthfuls and slipped off the bench, self-consciously teetering on wobbly legs. That's the last thing I remember. I don't know how they got me out of there, whether the whole town came to gawk or whether it was just Harmony and Vic and the waitress in the frilly uniform. I don't know who said what, or whether any of it was kind, or whether my mother might have cried that day.

* * *

I woke up slowly, my body numb as my mallet finger. All the gunk blistering beneath the surface had flushed itself out somehow. I thought how rage must hurt in the beginning, but a person gets so used to it, she thinks it's a heat a body's supposed to feel. Now I felt just a heaviness, like I'd been buried under the dirt. The sound of waves splooshed inside me, voices in the distance.

I opened my eyes and found myself in a bed with metal rails, a needle in my hand, fluid dripping from a bag.

"Why didn't you tell me you were sick?" The room was dark and Harmony looked awful, more pale than I'd ever seen. She looked smaller, too, her eyes enormous, framed by dark circles.

"I did."

"There's telling, and there's telling, Rebee." Harmony leaned in close, perched on the bed.

Vic wove in and out of the room, along with a smiley-button nurse named Gertie. Gertie said I had double pneumonia, which didn't mean I was twice as sick, only that both my lungs were infected. She said lots of thirteen-year-olds had walking pneumonia, a sickness so mild they don't even know they have it, but bad news for me, I didn't have the walking kind. My lungs were squawking like a barnyard of chickens.

A lady came in when I was alone behind the curtain. She smelled too sweet, lilacs maybe, and she was holding a basket like she was the Easter bunny. I pretended to be asleep.

The lady sat down in the armchair beside the bed and I cracked open one eye a smidge. Her basket was filled with sample packets, hand lotions I think, a tube of Vaseline and a couple of paperbacks with pink covers. She looked about the room, clucking and hemming. Maybe she expected balloons or stuffed bears.

Just as the lady stood up to pull back the curtains, Harmony came back, stopped cold and stared without blinking. The lady was so startled she crashed against the chair, her basket tumbling to the floor.

"Oh goodness," the lady said, because lotion packets scattered everywhere. The Vaseline tube slid under the tray table and she had to bend awkwardly and push it out with her shoe. She inched her way along the bed, stooping for all the stuff. Harmony watched, still as a statue, as the lady reached and scooped.

The lady was puffing from all that bending, but she straightened her flowery dress, stood up, and said, "I'm Ruthie. With the Hospital Pals. You must be Rebee's mother."

She held out her hand but Harmony didn't take it. Harmony didn't move.

"I've brought a basket for your daughter."

Harmony didn't acknowledge the basket. Or me either.

"It's what we do in this town," the lady added. "For new mothers. And our young patients." Then she smiled down at me, and I tried to prop myself up on my elbow.

"Hello there, Rebee," Ruthie said. "I've brought you a little something. From the town. A get-better gift."

"Rebee doesn't need anything from this town."

I'm sure no one had ever turned down a basket before, not in all Ruthie's years.

"You can go now," my mother said, waving her away. I tried to say thank you before the door wheezed shut, but my voice had rusted and nobody could hear.

* * *

After that, Harmony just hung onto my mallet-fingered hand, the one not attached to the tube. She must have taken bathroom breaks and she had to eat once in a while. But that's how I remember it. She held on tight for days.

Whenever Vic came into the room, the two of them would go at it. Right on top of me. Vic kept telling Harmony to grow up, to get herself help. Harmony told Vic to go back to her damn casino and leave the two of us alone.

A tube at the head of my bed gave off a yellowish light that blinked in and out. I kept my eyes shut.

The fog lifted, eventually. I remember waking with a start and craving toast so badly I could have cried for it. It was early morning, the sun behind the curtains coating the room like a crabapple peel, birds calling to each other at the window. Harmony was in the armchair beside my bed, her legs curled under her and one arm bent behind her head. We woke together and turned to each other at the exact same moment, and she climbed out of her chair and stretched out beside me, her head resting on the pillow facing mine. I was so shocked I held my breath, counting the seconds until I would wake up again and get it right.

"You scared me, Rebee," she whispered in my ear.

I didn't know what to say to her. After all my watching at some window, waiting for her to come back.

"I'm hungry," I said.

Harmony rolled away and stood. "Good. I'll see what I can scrounge up."

"Maybe some toast?"

She was dragging her fingers through her messy hair as she walked into the bathroom. "And strawberry jam?"

I couldn't see her, so I wriggled to a sit, my bruised hand still taped to its leash. "That would be nice," I said. When was the last time she'd asked me what I wanted?

I could hear the toilet flushing as I pulled the covers to my chin. When she came out, she'd splashed off any tenderness in the bathroom sink. She looked more like her old hard self. "We're leaving today," she announced from the doorway. "We've been here too long."

* * *

Harmony forgot about the toast. But Gertie came in with two slices, a big glass of orange juice and a bendy straw. I asked if I was allowed more, and she laughed, and said she would bring a whole loaf if that's what I wanted. I liked her Mickey Mouse watch. Her dark plum nail polish. How she smacked the pillows to puff them up.

In no time flat I had four more slices slathered in butter and jam. You'd think I was a half-starved dog.

She sat beside me on the bed. "Can we talk for a minute?"

She looked over her shoulder as if she might be caught. Where was my nail box? I could feel my face burn.

"There's a social worker stopping by."

I pictured Gertie's white runners, whisking in and out of the room without making a sound. She'd been doing it for days, me dribbling in my sleep.

"This afternoon. Before your discharge. Just to ask a few questions."

Gertie put her hand over mine, but I pulled it away and crammed a crust into my mouth. Then I remembered. My nails were hidden under the floor mat in Vic's back seat. No one would find them.

"Have you seen my mother?"

"I'm sure she's around." Gertie passed me my juice.

I guzzled through the straw until I sucked air.

"I think maybe I'll rest now," I said, crumpling my napkin on top of my toast plate.

"She'll want to talk to your mom, of course. The social worker. But she might want to talk to you, too." *I can't even imagine it*, her eyes were saying. "By yourself. Would that be all right?"

"Yeah, whatever." I pushed the tray back and flopped against my pillow.

"There are just a few things." Gertie would not get off my bed. "With your paperwork. Not a big deal."

"We've got money."

"No, no, nothing like that." She reached down, picked crumbs off my sheet with her plum nails. "It's about where you live, Rebee. Where you go to school."

Gertie kept tucking her brown curls behind her ear, but they kept springing loose. "Why don't you tell me about it? I've got time."

"I'm kind of sick of talking. But thanks anyway."

She stared at me, not budging, so I turned away and

mumbled into my pillow. "My mom and me. We talked all night practically."

All that toast inside me, pushing against my gown. "Like what I need for school. If I should take dance or piano. Whether we should get a dog."

What if nurses had X-ray vision and could actually see lies, rising warm and yeasty under a patient's gown?

"We do that all the time. Talk about stuff. Sometimes we make popcorn and crawl into bed and yak all night long."

I held my breath and waited. Finally, her weight lifted off the bed.

"Okay then," Gertie said. "You won't be needing this anymore." She slipped the needle out quick as anything and dragged the pole to the other side of the curtain. I didn't feel a thing. Just stared at my hand, as shrivelled as an old man's.

"She'll be coming by this afternoon. Clara Martin is her name. Have a little chat. And then you can go home."

I was dressed by the time Harmony came into the room. She looked used up, but relieved to see me sitting in the chair, runners tied, ready to bolt. My jeans and T-shirt seemed miles too big, like it was a different girl who stepped out of them a few days before.

On our trek to where Aunt Vic waited, smoking in the car, my legs shook so bad I thought I'd keel over. I looked back, in case Gertie watched behind the Emergency sliding door, but she'd moved on already, smacking the pillows in a real girl's room.

"I hate that hospital smell," Harmony said.

"Me too."

"Get it together, Rebee."

"I will."

“We’re not going to wind up in a place like this again.”

“We won’t.”

I didn’t know where we were going. But Harmony slowed down at least so we could walk side by side.

JOEY

THE OLD GUY NEXT DOOR OFFED HIMSELF IN HIS UPSTAIRS BEDROOM. Judge Shore was his name.

Not with a gun. Nobody's sure how. He was found dead in his judge's outfit and polished black shoes, sitting in the chair beside his made bed, eyes open, yellowish and filmy. They say he'd combed his bushy eyebrows and slicked down the strands of his white hair in a straight part to one side, and that his stiff fingers clutched the deed to his house. It was signed over to his granddaughter, Rebee Shore. At first, people thought he might have just expired dressed up like that — he was really old. Except that he pre-ordered that gravestone with the exact right end date, which was a pretty sure sign he had something fishy up his sleeve.

Rebee Shore showed for the funeral with her mom and her auntie. The three moved into the dead guy's house. Next door. Then the mom and the auntie moved out. Rebee Shore stayed. In between, there was yelling and swearing and stuff thrown all over the front lawn. People handle grief in their own ways.

* * *

I'm staying in Chesterfield with my grandma. Really. Chesterfield. It's just a pinprick on the map beside the wrinkly mountain. And she's not my real grandma. Everyone 'round here calls her Missus Nielson, even though there's never been a mister. Missus Nielson has managed to get hold of six Mixmasters and four toasters and twelve Nativity sets, but not one TV, not even one of those old styles with stickout knobs and rabbit ears. She's eighty-three years old. When my mom was a little kid, Missus Nielson looked after her, her first and last foster kid. I guess the whole motherhood thing didn't turn out like Missus Nielson hoped.

Motherhood isn't working too good for my mom either. Her name is Carla. It's her fault I'm in Chesterfield. Carla sent me here on my last day of school. I walked out of my Grade Eight classroom, and there she was, standing in the hallway, a Greyhound ticket in one hand and a new King James Bible in the other. She'd stuck three twenties under the King James flap — spending money for the rest of my life.

When she told me where I was going I nearly puked. "Missus Nielson's house? You're nuts." The last time I had seen Missus Nielson I was like five and she was a hundred. A herd of reindeer candy canes hung on her Christmas tree with pipe cleaner antlers and bows around their necks. Missus Nielson and Carla got into a big fight that day, and I had to polish off my turkey leg in the back seat of the car. I never even managed to swipe a candy cane.

"She's probably in a nursing home. What if she's dead?" I was pretty sure that lady didn't want her thirteen-year-old zit-faced no-relation fake grandson landing on her doorstep.

"Don't wreck this for me, Joey." My mother was off to save orphans in Africa. There would be no stopping her.

"You talked to her, right? Right?"

"Your grandma loves you. Jesus does, too."

"She's not my grandma. When are you coming back?" I knew her newfound calling wouldn't last, I just didn't know how many orphans it would take.

"Don't be a dick," Carla said. "It's a vacation. She's a real nice lady."

That's the last thing she said before she pushed me onto the Greyhound. Don't be a dick. I thought she might change her mind at the last minute. She does that all the time. Billy, that was Carla's most recent dumpee, Billy used to say stuff like, *Joey, that mother of yours is the kind of woman who has drunk, shot, popped, snorted, and laid every angle this side of China.* But when the bus driver slid the door shut, she slunk off quick as a wink.

I don't know how long this God kick of hers is going to last, but if you ask me, it's her worst try at a high yet. I'm so mad I could spit at those two guys in blue suits. They were the ones got her going. When they showed up at our door that first time they left a pamphlet. The second time they dumped four bags of groceries on our kitchen table. Then they took care of the gas bill and shovelled the sidewalk. The next thing I knew, we were sitting in the front pew, Carla freshly scrubbed, a picture of innocence, her string of tattoos submerged under a purple shawl and her fingers clutching the hymn book. Now she's off to Africa. Just like that.

The Greyhound actually stops in Chesterfield. There's no station. I got dumped on Main Street at the LetterDrop, which is like a post office, gift shop, card store, and bottle depot in one. The guy who runs it, Melvin Peevley, lives upstairs, and his supper smells pour out through the heat ducts and mix with the soap displays and the empty beer bottles people throw in the back room. Melvin also runs the funeral parlour, which is how I got the details about the polished boots and the combed eyebrows. Melvin says nearly the whole town showed up — Albert Shore being the circuit judge and all — and that the service was shorter than expected, just twenty-two minutes. The flowers were donated, snapdragons and delphiniums, plus a buggy bouquet of pink petunias. Melvin also says his *National Geographic*s date back to 1946, he prefers a gun with single-shot bolt action, and he thinks the ocean smells like wet dog.

Melvin Peevley has pale eyes and a large build and looks like he can't figure out where he belongs. He wears suit pants with moccasins, leaves his earring hole empty, cuts his hair short at the sides, but wears a funny-looking, too-skinny ponytail. He's got a moustache, too. When I told him I needed directions to find Missus Nielson's house, he said, *Well you got the right idea, son, cause that woman's sure not coming to you.* He went on to say she hasn't left her house, not in decades, except for one time when her back tooth abscessed and the auxiliary ladies covered her head with a towel when they drove her to the dentist's office. She gets everything delivered: her groceries and pills and *Reader's Digest* special offers. Chesterfield takes care of its own, yes it does.

Melvin offered to close down shop and drive me up to

Blueberry Hill. Really. That's what it's called. But I said, No thank you, Mr. Peevley, and headed out on my own. Missus Nielson's dilapidated house is beside the dead Judge Shore's at the end of a long winding oil road with nothing else around but trees and thistles. It takes twenty minutes from Main Street to get to the top of her hill, and that's hoofing it pretty good. That first day I puked twice on the way. Nothing substantial. There were no blueberries.

I rang her bell and then I banged on her door and then I let myself in. I think I expected Christmas, though now that I've settled in I imagine the candy canes are still here and I just haven't found them yet. There's crap everywhere. Newspapers piled higher than me. Shiny old lampshades with gold fringes. Cardboard boxes stacked like building blocks. Bags full of twist ties and elastic bands. Tiny wool balls no bigger than grapes. Cloth squares. Mandarin orange boxes filled with old photographs and scenes cut out from Christmas cards. Everything smells mouldy.

Missus Nielson coughed in the distance so I plowed ahead, tunnelling my way through the rows, inching forward a few steps, backing up, trying a different route. I found her in the kitchen.

She sat at a table covered with stacks of canned peas and waxed beans. I had no recollection of what she looked like. She's not what you would call flimsy. Her ankles are as fat as tree stumps. She's got wrestler's arms, puffy fists, and a large round head that sits like a balloon on top of her shoulders. She wears a little beaded purse on a chain around her neck, even when she goes to the bathroom.

She didn't see me at first. Her fingers were wrapped around a pair of orange-handled scissors, and she was trying to cut the lighthouse from the back page of a *Reader's Digest*. When she looked up, her scissors clattered to the table with a thunk.

"Grandma. It's Joey. Carla's kid. I'm here."

Her large head bobbed. I stared at the peas and waxed beans labels and all those cans bulging dangerously. She looked down at her lighthouse.

I lifted the plates and bowls off the chair next to her and put them on the floor beside a box of canning jars. She watched as I picked up the scissors and cut a perfect circle around the glossy scene.

"How's that?" I said.

After the lighthouse, I cut a square around the robins in the evergreen tree and a circle around the dove under the "Peace on Earth" greeting. From there, I just sliced into whatever she handed me.

¥ ¥ ¥

Things to do in Chesterfield. A — chuck the tennis ball on the shed roof, count the falling shingles; B — play Frisbee with the old 45 records from the box on the front porch; C — chuck the 45s on the shed roof, count how many stick.

When the excitement of A to C wears off, you can try for a coma. This involves lying in bed, lying perfectly still, breathing as little as possible, slower than slow, and transporting your body to where you won't wake up.

Grandma never interrupts. She's kind of sweet actually. Every time she peeks in my room, she goes, "Oooohhh," like she just remembered she's acquired me. She makes the exact same noises when she sees the baby Jesuses lined up in their porcelain cradles, like she doesn't know where they came from either.

But now there's the girl next door. She's in that big old house, all alone, using the same fork that poked the dead guy's tongue, sitting on the same toilet that once circled his butt. It's as good a reason as any to get out of bed. So now when Grandma starts shuffling around each morning, I do too. She does her bathroom stuff, then it's my turn. I drape my body over the stacked boxes to reach the taps, and then squeeze through the row of plastic-wrapped old lady dresses hanging along the shower curtain rod. There are seventeen shampoo bottles and eight soap-on-a-ropes.

Grandma makes bran muffins that taste like sawdust. I eat three. She says she's happy I'm here. She also says she's happy the town gives rebates to seniors for garbage disposal. She calls me a handsome young fellow, and I smile and say grandsonly things like "shucks."

There's a space about the size of an apple along the hedge between our houses where the leaves are brown and spindly. I can hunch down at this spot, invisible, and see everything going on. Yesterday Rebee Shore sat on her porch sipping root beer from a can and then she skipped down the stairs and onto her grass and kicked off her runners and laid down, arms spread wide, and stared up at the sky. Her ponytail fanned over the grass in waves. She was wearing a white blouse, the top three buttons open, and when the light sprung out from behind the clouds I could catch glimpses of her bra moving up and down, pressing against her skin. I stopped breathing and had to close my eyes. I don't know how long she lay like that because the taste filled my mouth and I needed to back away before I hurled.

Now at night, even when it makes perfect sense to aim for a coma, I lie there so horny I hurt. I listen to Grandma's snoring and picture Rebee Shore's small brown toes and open buttons and the way she stares at the sky like she's gonna win her showdown with God.

* * *

There's going to be an avalanche. We'll be flattened under a giant box slide, toasters and paint cans and coffee tins filled with screws raining down. This house is gonna cave with us in it. If I could get ahold of Carla, I'd tell her that even though she's one of God's children now, she's still a mom. I'd say, God is like the boss of social services and he's telling you to leave the orphans with the real missionaries and come get me.

When is she?

Where is she?

* * *

Down at the LetterDrop, Melvin Peevley sells painted wooden ducks for thirty-five bucks apiece. They look like tattooed chickens with birth defects.

I was trying to figure out how their beaks got so bent when Melvin snuck up on me. "Those there are Hank Haywood's ducks," Melvin said. "Local artist."

Melvin's moustache is really walrusy, a scattering of long, sharp-looking bristles.

"Can I buy some stamps, Mr. Peevley?"

"Melvin."

"That'll get to Africa?"

"Africa?" Melvin looked confused.

"Global postage, like for around the world," I said.

I thought about my letter. *Dear Carla: How are the orphans? Is diarrhea a problem? Are you really in Africa? If you're talking to God, please tell him I'm having strings of bad thoughts. Also, can you pass along your mailing address so I can send you this letter and we can sort out a few specifics? Like when I can get out of here?*

Melvin went back to the counter, hunched over and started rifling through drawers. "Lots of commotion up there on the hill. Those Shores coming back. Not that that lasted long. And damn but they left that girl on her own like that. Who knows when they'll come — " Melvin stopped midstream and looked up at me from the drawer. I think he just then made a connection between me and Rebee Shore. We were unexplainable landings. Like crop circles.

"So how's the girl?" he asked.

I shrugged and stared at my runners.

"Rebee Shore. Pretty girl. Right next door?"

I swallowed that taste in my mouth.

"Well, council's got their nose in it now. Worried about the legalities. She's only sixteen. A couple of the church ladies went up to see her, snoopy bunch, but she wouldn't let them in. They had to leave their casserole outside on the porch. I'd a liked to a seen that."

Melvin couldn't know, but I watched that little party from my hedge spot. There was also a pie. One lady was fat like an elephant and the other had Frisbee-sized earrings. The earring lady had a big voice. She used Okanagan cherries, she said, for the pie. Both ladies stood on their side of the porch landing and took turns grilling Rebee Shore.

Was she finding her way around Chesterfield all right? Was there anything they could help out with in her grandfather's house? Did she like tuna? Would she like to get picked up for church on Sunday? Each new question was louder than the last. By the end they were shouting, stealing desperate sideway glances at each other. Rebee never said anything as far as I could tell. She sure never opened her screen door. The big lady finally said, "Well, I guess we'll just leave this here then," and she bent over and put the pie on the porch, and then she climbed back upright, using the earring lady for a brace. After they huffed and puffed their way back to their car and drove off, Rebee threw the casserole in the garbage can by the road. But she ate the whole pie with her fingers out there on her porch. It was impressive.

Melvin found the right stamps and slid them over the counter. I fished out one of the twenties Carla left me.

"You need three," he said, counting out my change. "That's for a regular-sized envelope. So who you writing to in Africa?"

"A missionary," I said, turning to go.

"Cool." Melvin didn't know about Carla and the orphans. I'd told him I was in Chesterfield while my mother worked double shifts at the computer chip manufacturing plant in Edmonton.

"Thanks, Mr. Peevley."

"Melvin."

I turned back around again. "She gets to stay in the house, right? The Judge left it to her."

Melvin looked at me and smiled. "That's probably up to the mother. Calls herself Harmony now. What kind of a name is that?"

"Melodious," I offered.

Melvin snorted. "Well, my guess is that they'll sell and we can get back to normal around here."

"Great."

Melvin leaned toward me on his elbows. His breath smelled like coffee grounds. "There were two deaths in that same bedroom, you know. Albert's wife. She died in that room, too. A long time ago. Giving birth to that girl who calls herself Harmony now. That girl's real name is Elizabeth, same as her mother's. That poor woman — Elizabeth senior I'm talking about here — spent the day alone, struggling through labour." Melvin's voice dropped, barely a whisper, even though there was nobody else around and he'd probably hashed through these details with everyone in town.

"She didn't call for help." He shook his head as though he still couldn't believe it. "There was a bedroom phone right beside her, not an arm's length away, and she never even reached for it. Missus Nielson — your grandma, I guess you call her — well, she was looking after Victoria that day. That Victoria turned into one of those bad apple teenagers, didn't she just." He stopped, sniffing me over for bad apple smells. I passed the test, I guess, because he kept on going.

"Victoria was still a sweet wee thing — three or four maybe. The Judge was out of town like usual. Your grandma was the one who found her, the red wrinkled baby girl squawling between her legs, still attached to her umbilical cord. The one that calls herself Harmony now. Bloody mess that was. The Judge was never the same after that."

My stomach rolled with the picture, a ten-second warning, but Melvin kept yakking and I couldn't just run out like a girl. I tried not to breathe in his old coffee breath. Tried not to swallow.

"... wasn't right, a man alone in that house with those two little girls. Especially a judge. Your grandma took over, for a while anyway, until she and the Judge had a falling-out, over what, who knows. That woman can be as tight-lipped as a sky in a drought. No offence. We never saw much of him. Didn't get so much as a haircut in town, let alone contribute to the Kiwanis or the Chesterfield Improvement Fund. Indecent the way he stayed on."

I'd been backing up slowly and was almost at the door. "Thanks for the stamps, Mr. Peevley."

"Melvin. You want to know about those Shore girls, Joey, you ask your grandma."

It hadn't occurred to me I could ask Grandma. Ours was more of a moment-to-moment kind of relationship. What's a five-letter word for funny bone? Do you want more peas? Can you bring me that box? You mean that box there? That one there as big as a freezer in the fourth row beside the couch on top of the stack behind the other stack behind the pillows?

I made it to the alley and found a good place beside some tomato crates. Grandma's muffins come up easier than they go down. I've learned that you can't just duck into alleys and duck out again at the same spot. If anybody's around, they look at you weird. So I walked past the back of the shops until the alley ended and contemplated the goings-on in the house next door. Rebee's grandma lying in a pool of blood with Rebee's momma attached to a cord, like in *Alien*, only worse cause the blood was blood and not chocolate syrup and there was nobody yelling cut, great job, here's your zillion dollars. I wondered what Rebee Shore knew about her mom's landing on the planet. I hoped not much. For the first time ever, I felt glad I'd never nailed down the details about Carla's beginnings.

The alley ended in front of the Sugarbowl. It's a wooden shack beside Gaffy's Hardware, about as big as a bathroom, pink and white candy-stripe paint and a giant ice cream cone nailed to the roof. A girl with a dirty white apron and blue hair slid the window open as I came around the corner. She'd painted a thick black line around her eyes, which made her look mad. She was half out the window, gawking at me with those angry eyes. I didn't know what to do, so I asked if she had Tiger Tail ice cream. She slid the window back shut without answering. I wasn't sure if that meant yes or no, so I sat on the wooden bench in case. When she opened the window again, she passed me a cone wrapped in an already stained napkin, a lopsided blob of striped ice cream on top. She wanted to know if I was the new guy up on Blueberry Hill. I nodded dumbly. I wanted to know how she knew I was the new guy up on Blueberry Hill. So far, I'd only met Melvin. Maybe everyone knew everything about everyone in Chesterfield.

"Creepy about the Judge, right?" she said, twirling strands of blue hair tightly around her baby finger. "The whole town hated that guy." The dark stain down her front was shaped like a giraffe. The top of her apron hung open. Underneath, she looked even thinner than me. Starved, really. Her boobs just tiny little grapes.

"His place is haunted," she said matter-of-factly, like it was something I ought to know.

"Yeah, I know," I said.

"Really?" She picked up a bit, her painted eyes huge. She was old. Maybe sixteen.

"There's moaning and wailing," I said.

"Moaning and wailing!" She scratched at her apron like there were crawlies in there. "High pitched? Sorta aaaaah-hhhhh! Or is it more hissy and gaspy-sounding? Does she sound all pathetic and sad, or more like she's coming to rip your balls off?"

"Who?"

"The dead Judge's wife," like duh.

I nodded. I'm not good with small conversations. Or big ones. Nodding is a legitimate way to communicate. But then I thought of another thing to say. "It's complicated. The moaning. A lot of vocal range. Now it's the Judge, too, I think."

"Ohmigod. Like are they trying to communicate with each other? Doors slamming and stuff? You live right beside that asshole's house, right?"

My cone started to drip. I didn't want to swipe licks in front of her, so I just stood there and let the goop run down my fingers. "Yeah. It's pretty intense," I said, searching the window ledge for more napkins. There weren't any.

"Bet he'll never rest in shitty peace. He gave Chauncy Damer a two-year sentence for breaking into the Shauffers' barn and stealing a baby pig. Chauncy would have given that pig back, it was just a stupid bet with my idiot uncles, but the Judge threw him in jail anyway."

She leaned towards me on the window ledge and ran her fingers through her blue hair, lifting up chunks that were black underneath. I held my ice cream under the ledge so she wouldn't see the mess.

"Chauncy Damer ended up murdering a cab driver in Edmonton and now he's locked up again. So it's just you and Mrs. Nielson and the dead people up there on the hill?"

I nodded.

"Interesting," she said.

I guess she hadn't heard about Rebee Shore. I was glad somehow.

"Great place for a party," she added.

She slammed the window shut and I just stood there so she opened it again and said, "See you on the hill, Tiger," and then I backed away and started down the sidewalk. I dumped the cone in a flowerpot on Main Street and wiped my sticky hand on some guy's lawn beside a yellow dog turd. I was half way up the hill before it dawned on me that I shouldn't have said that stuff about the Judge's house. A party for the ghosts up there might not be a good thing.

* * *

After supper I decided to test Melvin Peevley's theory about Grandma remembering stuff. We'd finished our pink pork chops and canned peas and she was leaning into the sink in her flowery housecoat, that's all she ever wears, that and the little beaded purse she hangs around her neck. I asked if she would tell me about the Judge. She had her back to me, rinsing off our gnawed-off bones for the bag in the freezer. That's another thing she hangs onto. Gnawed-off bones. When she didn't say anything, I tried asking again, giving clues. The Judge your neighbour, the guy who died in his bedroom a couple of weeks ago, the fellow whose little girls you used to look after, the man the town despised. She stopped washing my pork chop bone and held it up high, like a sword, and stared out the window. Finally I gave up and went into my room and restacked the boxes along the wall into an Autobot Transformer.

One minute I was lying on top of the dusty quilt, eyes closed, wondering which would hurt more, being shot in the ear with a BB gun or stung by a horsefly, and then Grandma's standing over me like a ghost in the dark.

"She used to suck on the middle two fingers of her left hand," Grandma said. "She'd pop them out for a second, just long enough to say a few words or eat a cookie, then back they'd go."

"Oh Kay," I said. Grandma had three pink curlers on the top of her head. This was her nighttime outfit. She still had that beaded purse around her neck.

"She suckled those poor little fingers so hard they were shrivelled and stained as old pickled beets."

"Do you know where you are, Grandma?" I swung my legs over the side of the bed and sat up straight. There were four clocks in my room, but none of them worked. It felt like the middle of the night, mostly because who has this kind of conversation in broad daylight.

"I tried all sorts of tricks to break her sucking habit," Grandma said, continuing. "Soaking her fingers in vinegar, binding her hand in cotton strips, bribing her with mint jellies or paper cutout dolls."

"Uh huh," I said Maybe Grandma was sleeptalking. Maybe I should go round the house and try to make a safe route for her.

"Nothing worked. He was furious with us both. *Get that girl to quit gnawing on herself. It's obscene to watch.* But then one day she simply stopped. Just like that. She said, 'I don't have to help them anymore.' And that was the end of the finger sucking."

Grandma smiled, half chuckling to herself.

"I'm glad that worked out then," I said.

"Oh, she was like that. Elizabeth. Once she made up her mind about something, she never turned back."

Elizabeth. I thought about that lady outside the Judge's house after the funeral, a more grown-up version of Rebee. "You mean Rebee's mom?"

Grandma looked confused when I asked that, though not more than usual, and it was hard to tell in the dark.

"Rebee's mom. That Elizabeth?"

Grandma nodded slowly, painfully it seemed. "She looked nothing like Albert, or her sister Victoria, either. That's what started the talk, Elizabeth skipping along the sidewalk in her taffeta dress and patent leather shoes. There was no question she was her mother's child. Those busybodies around here couldn't see anything of Albert in her."

Grandma looked old and frail, remembering the little girl. I pictured Rebee's almond eyes, like her mother's. Her grandmother's too, apparently.

"I think you should sit down, Grandma. Here, sit."

"That poor lost girl. I should have done more."

Who was lost? But Grandma had turned herself around, feeling her way back to bed.

* * *

About a month into school last year I asked Mr. McCormick, the gym teacher, if I could be excused. Normally, he said, sure, sure, be quick about it, but his wife and kids divorced him that week, moving as far away as they could get without a passport — Nova Scotia, I think — and they took his German shepherd Wally, too. Mr. McCormick loved that dog. He was in a crappy mood and said that I could do my business before gym class started and why didn't I grow some balls and climb the frigging rope already. I made it halfway up. The stream landed like a bowl of broken eggs on top of Mr. McCormick's bald head.

It's embarrassing to puke on your gym teacher. This morning was worse. When Rebee leaves the hill, she doesn't just meander down the road into town. She straps herself into a giant backpack like she's planning to hike across Canada. Then she takes the hard way, out back of our houses, which is straight down through the trees. I've seen her go this route a dozen times. Sometimes she's gone for an hour. Sometimes all day. Sometimes she brings home a carton of eggs or a six-pack of root beer. Sometimes she leaves with her hair in a ponytail and when she comes back, it's falling around her face.

So this morning I followed her over the cliff and down into the forest. It's dark like night in there. Very creepy. There's a broken wooden gate growing out of the ground. And a burned tree that looks like a woman praying. It's got fat knots in the wood for her boobs and two thick branches like arms reaching to God.

I was doing pretty good, keeping my distance, clambering over the fallen logs and moss-covered rocks, like Spider-Man without the suit. But I got so busy looking ahead, trying to keep her in sight, that I missed a tree root and went careening down the hill, head over ass. A tree stopped my fall, eventually, and I lay there panting, bark chips and needles stuck to my shirt. When I opened my eyes, Rebee stood over top of me. I'd never been that close to her before. She wore a purple tank top and jeans that sat low on her hips and she stared at me without blinking.

"Hello," I said, my first word. Ingenious.

She didn't answer. Just stared. It made it hard for me to pretend that I'd skied down the hill on my ass on purpose. I hoisted my top half onto my elbows and tried to look casual.

"You're bleeding," she said, pointing to my forehead.

"What?" I raised my palm to my head and felt the lumpy wet, and when I brought my hand down it looked like it had come out of a bowl of tomato soup with pepper. There was no warning. Not even a millisecond. The volcano erupted and I spewed. It was like orange Slurpee when you yank on the handle too hard. I thought to lean to the side, eventually, but by then it was all over, and I daintily spit the last few blobs into the soggy leaves. I must have looked like a kid's drawing. I had a bloody red hand from touching my bloody head, and now orange watery puke all down my shirt, mixing nicely with the green forest bits I'd picked up on my way down.

I didn't dare look up. All I could see were her scuffed runners sinking in moss less than a foot in front of me. They hadn't backed up an inch. Most people gag, or cover their mouths, or jump to a safe distance to escape the explosion. Rebee just stood there in front of me. I wanted her to be gone. I wanted her to back down the hill and melt into the trees so I could disappear off the planet. I looked at my gooey shirt, looked at my runners, looked at her runners, looked at the ants marching along the log, looked for something else to look at.

She asked, "Can you stand up?"

I remained perfectly still, trying not to pant, trying to ignore my dripping head.

"Well?" There was a hard edge to her voice. No pity. Those that stuck around were usually the "oh dear, poor puking boy" types. Big hair ladies, mostly. Rebee had none of that.

"You can go," I said. "I'm gonna just hang out for awhile."

She was on her knees then. She had swung her heavy backpack off her shoulders and it landed on the ground with a thunk. It was a blue deluxe model, the kind that prepares you for anything, with outside pockets handy for water bottles or wet shoes, and a rear pocket big enough for a folding avalanche shovel. I wanted to be dead, but I wanted to see inside more. When she opened the main zipper and started rooting around, I snuck a peek. It looked like everything she owned had been crammed in there. Jacket, T-shirts, a cracked mirror with a shiny frame, two rubber boots, a couple of apples, even a nightie. I thought she was going to pull out an IV bag, but her fist dived down and came back up with a tattered roll of Life Savers. Wintergreen. She popped two in her mouth without offering me one.

"You travel prepared," I said. I waited for her to say something like yeah, I know, or, what brings you to this neck of the woods. She didn't. So I said, "I know who you are."

"So do I."

I wished I could hang myself from the nearest branch. "I mean, I — I live next door. Just temporarily, probably the summer. I'm Joey. My grandma used to look after your mom, when she was just a little girl. Elizabeth."

She looked at me hard and I bit my tongue to stop myself

from turning away. The tip of her booger finger was bent under in a weird, E.T.-come-home way.

She said, "Her name is Harmony." She passed me the Wintergreens, and when I reached out with my non-bloody hand, I could smell the reek of me fill the forest.

"I stink."

"You do." She sat down and crossed her legs, pulling the backpack onto her lap.

"Sorry I puked."

But she had her head in her backpack and was sorting through her stuff.

"I'm sorry your grandpa died." Wasn't I just full of apologies. "I never met him. I'm sure he was a great guy."

Her head popped out of her bag again. "Here." She was holding a folded white T-shirt in her fist.

I wasn't going to put on a girl's shirt. I shook my head. "Thanks anyway."

"Like you said. You stink." She dropped the shirt in my lap.

"I'm leaving now," I said, trying to pass her back her shirt. "Sorry."

"Put it on. Unless you want pink."

She almost smiled. But there was something else, too. Something tight and ninja-like. My skin felt shivery as we sat there staring at each other in the shadows.

I really stunk. I thought I might be sick again just having to breathe me in. So I fumbled with my shirt buttons, hoping she would find a hedge to hide behind or that she'd at least look away, but she sat cross-legged in front of me and watched. I crunched up my puked shirt like a dirty diaper and hucked it over by a tree. By the time I got my scrawny white arms and puny pounding chest and pathetic protruding ribs into Rebee's shirt, she was pouring water from a plastic water bottle over a piece of cotton.

It took a few seconds for the horror to pass. She was handing me a wet mini pad and pointing to my forehead. I swiped a few times until the pad was covered with brown red blood and pebbly grit, and Rebee held out her hand and took it from me. She rolled it like a cigarette and stuffed it into the avalanche shovel pocket and passed me another. And another. And another. I thought we might do an entire box's worth, but we stopped at four.

"It's just a scratch," she said. "Can you stand up?"

I didn't want to appear helpless, not after spitting up like a baby and passing blood-soaked mini pads back and forth, so I jumped right up.

"Well, that was fun," I said, sliming my hand up and down my jeans.

"Do you want me to walk with you up the hill?"

"No, no, no," waving my arms like I was on fire. "I'm all right. Really."

"I know," she said. "Right as rain."

We both stood and brushed ourselves off and I turned and looked up the hill and took in my impressive skid marks in the moss. Every tree looked the same except for the praying lady, standing out like a scorched thumb. Rebee must have followed my eyes, because she mumbled, *Harmony's tree*, but didn't explain.

"Weird how it could somehow burn itself up without starting the whole forest on fire," I said.

"Whatever. It's dead."

She swung her backpack high like it was as light as air

and adjusted the straps on her shoulders and said, "See you, Joey."

"Sorry for the trouble," I said. Idiot.

But by then she was gone.

¥ ¥ ¥

The gash looks like an upside down purple V above my left eyebrow, a "this way up" arrow for dummies. It will probably leave a scar, a handy reminder that I'm a piece of turd. A part of me hopes it's permanent. Maybe when I look in the mirror from now on I'll only see her.

Grandma was really sweet to me when I came out of the bathroom. I was surprised her old eyes picked up on my scruffiness, that she could see how my forehead was even puffier than hers. She poured me a glass of funny-smelling milk and told me to sit and rest.

I slumped at the kitchen table.

"You have to be more careful when you play outside," Grandma said, patting my elbow.

"I was with Rebee, Grandma. Rebee Shore." Just a regular barf fest back there on the hill.

Grandma shuffled out from behind me and sat down heavily at the table. "Rebee Shore. Elizabeth's child? She's a nice girl?"

Nice was not quite the word. "Yeah, she's nice."

"And Elizabeth. Has she gone then?"

I didn't want to get into the whole Harmony name change thing. "Yeah, she's gone." Coincidentally, so was Carla.

"She didn't come to see me," Grandma said.

"Maybe she thought. . ." *you were dead*. But I stopped

myself and said instead, ". . . thought you'd go see her. At the old — at the Judge's funeral. Or afterwards. Like, next door. Maybe she doesn't know you don't get out much anymore, Grandma."

Grandma nodded as though she were thinking how maybe she didn't get out as much as she should. "I was glad when Elizabeth left here. And she raised that child right. She's a nice girl?"

She really wanted Rebee to be a nice girl. "You were glad Rebee's mom left? How come? Chesterfield being such a swell place and all."

"That house next door."

I fidgeted in my chair, waiting for her to spit it out. She moved the top peas can to the wax bean row. I was afraid she'd start rearranging the vegetables, which could take all week.

"What about the house next door," I yelled.

"It was a long time ago. I'm an old woman now."

She was an old woman then. "Sounds like the Judge was an asshole."

I shocked her into dropping her hand to her lap.

"Everybody says so, Grandma. The whole town."

"This town loves its tittle-tattle." She stamped her slippered foot under the table. It was a slow motion stamp, but it came down hard enough that it probably hurt. "They're a hungry bunch hoping for a nibble of anything repeatable. I will not give them the satisfaction of speaking about Albert that way."

"Whoa," I said. She had gotten herself worked up all of a sudden. Her lips were sweating.

"Albert loved his wife. Elizabeth."

"Okay. I believe you."

“Albert kissed the ground she walked on. They used to stroll down Main Street with Victoria, first a bundle in Albert’s arms, then toddling between them in her frilly sun-frocks and matching bonnets. Back then, everyone would say there goes the Judge and his lovely wife.”

Weird. Hearing my grandma talk about Rebee’s grandma like that, the lady that died in the bedroom next door, like she might float by the window and wave hello. Her name was Elizabeth, too. Rebee’s grandma, Rebee’s mom. It seems stupid to me when families do that — Bob Senior, Bob Junior, Bob Baby Junior — like they’re A&W burgers. Victoria, the kid in the frilly outfit — that would be Rebee’s auntie, the scary one with the long black hair and skin-tight jeans. The one who drove the Shore girls up the drive after the funeral and then stomped back and forth from the porch to the car for three days yelling stuff to Harmony like, “Goddamn bitch,” and, “Least the old fucker had the decency to end it,” and to Rebee, “You’re getting out of this hell hole if I have to drag you by your hair.”

Grandma missed all that ruckus.

“So he was a great guy,” I said. “The Judge. A nice little family.”

Grandma looked up at me rather harshly, as if she didn’t know whether she should go on. I nodded to her encouragingly.

“It crept up on them slowly — the town. How Elizabeth had stopped showing herself, how the Judge was walking down Main Street alone, going about his business, not bothering to tip his hat or inquire as to everyone’s health. They all wanted to know what went on in that house those months before Elizabeth died.”

"So," I said. Waiting. "What went on?"

Grandma rocked back and forth in her creaky chair, head down, chins bobbing.

"Bad business."

Bad business. What did that mean? The Judge? Maybe he was a great guy until he had a little vodka in him, all buddy buddy, joking around, and then he'd turn, mean as a snake, and throw you into a wall.

The sky outside the window looked dull and grey. I touched the gash on my forehead and sat shivering in the sweltering kitchen.

Grandma stopped her rocking. "Albert was decent." She looked at me, really looked at me. Her glasses were covered with splotches, but her eyes were clear and soft inside their wrinkled pouches. "He was a man with a broken heart. A man like that, his world cracks open. Don't let them tell you otherwise."

She stood slowly, leaning on the table, and limped towards the counter. She poured the black liquid from the teapot into her cup.

"Do your knees hurt?"

"These old aching bones," she said, her back to me. Then she stared out the window and slurped her cold tea. "I wished she would have come to see me."

Well, she's gotta come back, I thought. She left her kid here. Mothers can't just dump their kids and not come back.

* * *

After my freakshow in the forest, I stayed clear of the hedge spot. I didn't want to run into her again. It was almost worth the puking incident to have her blazed to the back of my eyeballs, the picture where she's lying in the grass with her breasts pointed up. I didn't want to wreck it by seeing what she sees when she looks at me.

I did scrub my knuckles raw on Rebee's XSMALL made in India 100 percent cotton T-shirt, using scoops of blue-speckled laundry detergent from one of the three six-gallon drums stacked in Grandma's hallway. By the time I got done, it looked white as milk, all traces of puke gone. I wrapped the T-shirt in tissue I found in one of Grandma's shoeboxes of crinkled paper. My plan was to wait for a cloudy night. After Grandma did her curlers and got settled in bed, I would cleverly sneak over to Rebee's doorstep and leave the T-shirt on the landing, same as that dropoff cherry pie.

I chose a perfect night, so still and dark up here on Blueberry Hill the whole world seemed to have sucked itself down a black hole. Rebee's lights were off, and I stared out my bedroom window and tried to guess which room she slept in, whether she wore panties under her nightie. Grandma kept shuffling into the bathroom and flushing. When she finally started snoring, I was a bundle of nerves. I did one planned puke in the toilet, then stuffed my bony arms into my black hoody and tiptoed around the obstacle course of boxes and stepped out into nothingness. I felt my way along my side of the hedge, stretching my arms out like a zombie. Every few steps I'd get whapped in the face with a sticky branch and have to straighten myself out again. When the hedge ran out and my feet hit gravel, I turned around, and slunk back along her side of the overgrown clumps. I made it to her porch step without hearing any stomach rumbles, or feeling the Judge's dead fingers clawing down my pants. So far so good, I thought.

"Hello, Joey."

I squealed, an octave higher than possible, flinging my arms, and Rebee's T-shirt, high into the night.

Rebee sat on the porch step, small as a baby bird, arms hugging knees. My heart stopped beating. What was she doing out there all alone in the pitch black when a perfectly good house stood right behind her? I wanted to run — run far, far away — but my legs were rubber. So was my penis.

"Do you know how to drive?" she asked.

That was her question? Not, "What the crap are you doing on my porch in the middle of the night? or "How come you scream like a kindergarten girl?" I mumbled something incoherent about my excellent driving skills.

Rebee stood, lightning fast. She was wearing a white blouse and a flimsy little sweater. I could feel the whites of her eyes, a flash of teeth, her wintergreen breath. Then she seemed to float down the steps and pass on by into the soupy night. "Come on," she commanded, like I was her dog. Like a dog, I followed.

We ended at the garage — a rundown version of the grandfather's house, only smaller. Peeling white sides and a green roof. It sat close to the cliff at the back of the property, so saggy a good kick might push it over the edge. That building was creepy enough at lunchtime, let alone on a night like this.

She said, "If a van's in there, I'll smash all the windows."

I stood frozen to her side. I wondered what weapon she'd use and whether she'd be able to stop smashing once she started. She jiggled the handle and the door cracked up an inch and she got her fingers underneath and yanked, so I did too. It took considerable heaving, but when the door finally squealed upwards a rush of musty air escaped. Gasoline and wet rag and old man and other smells crawled up my nose. I stumbled back a few steps, trying to get away, but I only had a few seconds before I bent over and retched, a symphony of dry heaves, loud enough to wake all of Chesterfield. Rebee peered into the garage, ignoring my hullabaloo. Then she disappeared inside. I was empty before I started, just spit lumps, and when I finally got upright I stepped inside too. A shiny silver car took up nearly the whole garage. It was one of those old-fashioned pointy types with a great wide hood and fins like wings that could launch into space. I stood in front of it, my hand clutched over my nose, and watched Rebee open the car door and slip in behind the steering wheel. I thought, this is how a deer in the headlights feels, except without the headlights. It occurred to me she might start the engine and floor the gas. But then she leaned across the seat and the passenger door creaked open, and I felt a flood of relief, partly because I was still alive, but mostly because she didn't expect me to drive us out of there.

I squeezed myself into my side of the car, closed the door, and buckled my seatbelt, which was a waist-only kind like airplanes have. First I thought, well that's great, if we get in an accident I'll be sliced in half. Then I thought, idiot. There were no keys in the ignition. I'd never sat in anything like it. An antique for sure, like the Judge. The dashboard was jukebox glitzy, polished; the steering wheel round and skinny, like a bicycle tire. Everything was spotless, as if no fingers had touched anything. The smell was bearable, pleasant even, just a faint trace of old man cologne mixed with Rebee.

"Nice car," I said. Rebee said nothing. She stared straight ahead, like we were driving down a highway. It was black out there. The world had disappeared. "I wonder what kind of mileage this thing gets."

Her eyes were on some imaginary road, oblivious to everything, including me. Her little sweater was unbuttoned and from my side view I could see the points of her nipples pressing against her white blouse. I looked down to be sure the folds of my hoody hid the raw potato sprouting in my pants.

I didn't know what she wanted me to do, but it got too hard to just sit there and imagine her and keep my mouth shut. "I guess this car used to belong to your grandpa. Doesn't look like he's driven it in a while. Right. Sorry. He's dead. Of course not. Sorry. But good for him that he kept up the maintenance."

I couldn't stop. I prattled on, same as Grandma when she's doing her cutouts.

"The rides I'm used to are more — disorganized," I said. "Cracked windows, beer bottles, Timmy's cups. You know, cigarette butts, burger wrappers, that kind of thing."

Rebee ran her finger in a circle around the skinny steering wheel and I couldn't help staring at the way it curled over at the end, like a claw.

"Billy, that's my mom's last boyfriend, he kept a deer head in the truck named Ned." My hair was sweaty and my ears prickled. "Ned had his eye gouged out and a broken antler and a red scarf around his neck."

I was mesmerized by her finger going round and round. I wondered if she'd trained it to bend over like that. "I don't know how his antler snapped in half, whether it was before or after he got shot, and whether it hurt, or if it was more like when your nail rips off at the tip, and you don't even notice until you try to scratch something."

She turned to me, and when I finally tore my eyes away from her crooked finger she said, "Seen enough?" Then she made a fist and pressed it into her stomach like a slow motion punch.

I felt dumb as a truck. Sweat trickled down the sides of my arms. I didn't dare look at her. Then I felt even dumber because I thought maybe I'd embarrassed her into hiding her finger in her stomach.

"I have a really ugly birthmark on my thigh," I blathered, my voice cracking. I felt fluttery, not the jolt to the stomach kind, but an all-over lightheadedness, like if I wasn't wearing a seatbelt, I would float into space. "It looks like a giant purple starfish. Carla says it's because my daddy was sea scum. I'm sure somebody was sea scum, but who knows who's who. Does your mom have boyfriends?"

I think she shook her head no. It moved slightly.

"You're lucky. Carla's don't last. A couple of times we moved in. This one guy had a monster dog that lived in a car in his backyard. The car had a dangling back door and the dog spent his days sprawled out on the shredded back seat, panting."

She was looking out the window again, popping a Wintergreen behind her pink lips, passing me the package.

"I did a spreadsheet once." I fumbled with the wrapping. When the Life Saver hit my tongue, the mintiness nearly bowled me over. "For possible matches. I was planning to cross-reference my personality traits against every gook Carla looked at. If a guy puked after a binger, he'd get a tick. Skinny arms — tick. A sick fear of rodeo clowns — tick. But then I started making stuff up and it was tick, tick, tick. It just got too weird."

Rebee laughed, a throaty raw sound. "Every kid without a dad makes up stuff about a dad," she said.

She was actually talking to me. "Did you?" I asked.

"Sure."

"Like what?"

She sighed. "I don't know." I figured that was that, but then she said, "We met a man at a campground once. There was snow."

I wasn't sure if I should ask questions. Like did she build a campfire? Did smoke get in her throat? Were there marshmallows on a stick? Did they make her stomach cramp?

We just sat there. I thought, well, at least your mom took you camping, but I couldn't say that. I could feel Carla's *stop your whining* smack on the side of my head.

"He took Harmony for a drive in the middle of the night," she said finally.

"And not you?" I asked.

She looked straight ahead. I guessed that meant no.

"Afterwards, I made up stuff. I might have pretended he was my father."

"Well, at least he brought your mom back. Obviously. That was good."

She didn't say anything.

"Were you scared?" No, of course not.

"Maybe a little. Not so much. Not when he took her

away. Just when he brought her back and everything stayed the same."

I didn't know what she meant, not really, so I asked, "Did he say sorry?" He should have, I thought.

She shook her head. A piece of her hair fell onto her cheek. "We disappeared. I don't think about him any more."

"Maybe he's still looking for you?" If I were that guy, I'd still be looking for her.

"Right," she said.

"Don't you still want to find him?"

She shrugged. "It was just kid's stuff. That's what kids do. They make stuff up."

"What about your real dad. Don't you want to know?"

Rebee swivelled and looked straight at me. I blinked several times because her eyes looked icy cold and she didn't look away. "My father's dead," she said finally. She seemed more angry than sad.

"That's crappy," I stuttered. "Maybe my dad's dead too."

"There's worse things than not knowing, Joey."

"Okay." I nodded dumbly.

I looked about, feeling awkward. The garage doorway had become an open mouth wanting to swallow us into the black night. I thought of what might be hiding under the rocks up there on the hill. A thousand pair of eyes stared in. If a creature pounced on the hood, she might expect me to do something. I shuddered and edged my arm up the side of the door and popped down the lock.

Then, out of the blue, she said, "It's harder than I thought it would be."

"What's harder?" I was hoping she didn't mean me.

"Staying in one place."

"Oh." According to my count, she'd been in Chesterfield all of twenty-one days. "I guess you and your mom move around a lot?"

"Yes. A lot."

"Everything moves in slow motion here," I said. "It takes Grandma all morning just to get down the hall. How long are you staying at your grandpa's?"

"Perpetually."

"Like in forever?"

"Exactly."

"On purpose?" I couldn't imagine anyone with choices staying in Chesterfield.

She nodded and said quietly, "But it's hard."

I thought she sounded sad. I didn't want to point out that she was being illogical. With all the comings and goings after the Judge's funeral, I was pretty sure *she* was the one telling the grownups she'd stay, not the other way round. Seems to me, she could change her mind. *Hey, Mom. Thought I'd like it here. Turns out, it sucks. Come get me.* Carla says girls' thoughts are like spit; they don't change so much as evaporate. But Rebee didn't seem vaporous. She seemed like the kind of girl who grabbed hold of an idea and it stuck.

I wanted to say something bright, but nothing came to me. It was getting colder, the air in the car breathlessly quiet. It felt like something was out there, coming for us.

"You must be used to new places," I said with gusto. "With all your moves. That's good. And you get out and about a fair bit. That's better than being in a coma. Not that I'm spying or — "

"I used to pretend I was ready for anything. But this is

the end of the road, and I can't think of what the anything might be."

I was utterly without an idea of what my anything might be either. I was thinking this could be it. We stared straight ahead into the shadows and sucked on our Wintergreens.

I'm not that experienced with women, except for Carla and Grandma and a string of lady teachers that I've managed to avoid making eye contact with. Oh, and there was the ice cream girl encounter, the one I would have replayed a thousand times if I hadn't already had Rebee in my head. But here I was, sitting in a dead man's car beside the most amazing girl of all girls in the world, and she wasn't even trying to get away.

A wind rose all of a sudden, hard and mean, whistling through the window cracks. Some heavy broken thing clattered against the garage roof. Clank. Klump. I hoped it wasn't Rebee's grandpa. Or grandma. Or anything dead. Or anything alive either.

"Do you believe in ghosts?" I asked. I was in way over my head.

"It's just the wind."

"Yeah, I know that."

She hugged the steering wheel and rested her chin over top. My waist was still mashed against the seatbelt, but I'd shrivelled back down to my normal shrivelledness, so I tugged at the clasp and sprung myself loose. I stretched out my legs and leaned against the Judge's car door to face her.

"Seems like you could do anything you wanted," I said above the whomp, whomp, whomp of the trees. Strangely, my stomach didn't hurt at all, which worried me a little.

Rebee turned to me and almost smiled. "I don't know how to drive."

"Me neither," I confessed, rather too quickly.

Rebee examined me closely. "You've got time."

"We only do beaters. Our last had a flat tire. Carla left it on the side of the road, got on a bus, and never went back."

Rebee took her Wintergreen out of her mouth and held the tiny white round sliver on the tip of her finger. Then she flicked her tongue and it disappeared.

"Harmony can change a flat in less time than it takes to lick the powder off a Fun Dip stick. We have a van. We've always had a van. The Judge took care of that."

"Vans are expensive. He must have been generous." *Vans are expensive.* I was such a dork.

Rebee shivered and hugged herself. The car was cold as a refrigerator. The wind was actually screeching through the window cracks.

"Did you like him? Your grandfather?"

Grandma called him a decent fellow. Broken-hearted, but decent.

"The Judge? We never met. But he gave us money. Regular as alimony. Harmony made her living by stepping up to a bank machine."

It didn't seem that bad, having her grandpa pay the rent every month. It was better than a church. Running off to save orphans.

"Harmony could drive for hours and hours. She never got lost. Sometimes she'd pull over on some stretch of back road and tell me to take over."

"Did you?"

She shook her head.

"At least she taught you to drive."

Rebee laughed her throaty laugh. I would recognize the sound of it anywhere.

"God no," she was saying. "But I'd watched her since I was a kid. That should be enough."

"I got into an accident once when we were parked at the Liquor Barn," I said. "Carla was inside, buying booze. I stayed in the car. It was parked on a hill, sheer ice, and the car started sliding backwards in slow motion. I hit an old man in a station wagon." I actually had my head between my legs, and when we thumped, I made a bite mark on my knee, but Rebee didn't need to know that part.

"Were you okay?"

"Yeah. The old guy told Carla to shut the hell up, that if she couldn't figure out how to put on the emergency brake, how was her kid supposed to."

Rebee looked at me closely. "It wasn't your fault."

I swallowed. I never imagined an older girl like this. I've imagined a lot of girl stuff, but not sitting across from one and talking. I didn't have the least inkling to barf.

I blurted, "So if your Mom wanted you to drive so bad, she should have taught you." Carla would have said, *What do you expect, a fucking Mother Teresa?* Well, the pre-Jesus Carla would have said that. Now she'd probably say, *God go with you, my son.*

"Harmony would crawl in the back, and I'd just sit there and stare at the dangling key. Then I'd get out and trudge up and down the road and kick at rocks and wait for her second wind to blow us to the next town."

"Oh," I said.

After that, we sat for a while and didn't say anything and

listened to the wind all around us. The windows fogged and my toes felt numb. Rebee seemed sad, lost in her own little world. I wanted to make her laugh again, come up with something funny — maybe a story about Grandma's bone collection — but my nose started to run and I couldn't concentrate.

I was using my sleeve when it happened. I'll never forget. She crawled across the seat and buried backwards into my hoody and pulled her legs up close so that all of her leaned into my chest. I could smell her cucumber hair and Wintergreen breath and I put my arms around her shoulders and tried not to touch her breasts and she pressed harder into me and I could feel her shivering and my heart thudding against her sweater and I held on tighter and rested my chin on the top of her head and my lips accidentally touched a piece of her hair and I kept my eyes wide open and looked down and could see her breasts like apples and I thought for sure I would explode because this was really happening. This was not my hand wrapped around my dick. This was Rebee and she was a real girl and she was completely beautiful.

"I can hear the highway in my head," Rebee said after awhile, her voice muffly in my shirt.

"It's okay," I said. "It's the wind."

"We're okay," she said.

I don't know how long we stayed like that. A long, long time. I woke up shivery, hugging myself, neck crinked, skin prickling with goose pimples. Sometime in the night, she'd disappeared. I didn't even feel her go. I stumbled out of the car into the morning's quiet breeze. Birds chirped happily. A pair of squirrels chased each other. The sky had little pink swirls. Everything was where it was supposed to be.

The house, the hedge, the cracked empty birdbath. If there weren't twigs and branches thrown about, you'd have never guessed a wind had howled through there.

* * *

But I know I didn't imagine her. Rebee left four hairs on my hoody. One is as long as my arm from my elbow to my wrist. It's soft and shiny and sparkles in the sun.

Carla says a girl will watch a boy drown and then step on his head. Maybe she's right. I feel like I'm drowning. Rebee won't talk to me. I don't know what I did wrong. It's been three days.

That first day I knocked on her door. Then I sat on her porch step and waited. There was the sound of a chainsaw in the distance. Then it stopped. The mosquitoes came and I slapped at my arms. The chainsaw started. The air smelled too summery, like dirt and dandelions. I barfed a little in the mossy stuff beside the porch. I wandered over to her grandpa's garage and stared in at her grandpa's car and listened for the sound of her voice, but there was nothing but the faraway chainsaw and a few crickets and a caw, caw, cawing crow in the white sky. So I sat in the car where she sat and smelled her clean cucumber smell. I traced my fingers everywhere hers had been. Then I leaned into the horn with my head and held it there and listened to the tinny beep bounce off the walls. After a while I got out of the car and tugged on the garage door and watched it fall sticky slow. I went back to the porch and knocked on her door. When I felt too dizzy to stand in one spot, I sat on the porch step some more. A breeze came up over the tops of the trees and the leaves swirled a bit and the mosquitoes went away. I dozed and woke with a start and barfed a little more on top of a different piece of spongy ground. The crow lifted from the tree, circled on top of my head, then landed back on the branch, hopped to its tip, and stared back at me. The sun shifted and the shade on the porch disappeared, and I just sat there and fried.

I did it all over again yesterday, except there was no chainsaw and I didn't honk the horn and I was covered with mosquito bites and my ears and forehead burned. And there were clouds shaped like baseball caps roaring across the busy sky and a few rain splats in the afternoon.

Grandma found a bottle of children's vitamins in one of her boxes in the living room. She said they would make me right again. I stared at the bottle until the letters turned fuzzy. According to the lid's date, I was twenty-five years too late.

"I'm sorry, Joey." She cleared her throat as though something stuck in there. One hand covered the other, like she was holding a dying bird. "I'm sorry," she said again.

I didn't know what she was sorry for. I hadn't told her about Rebee. I hadn't said one word about drowning inside. About feeling how maybe for the first time in my life I'd found something to hang onto, but now I had just a sinking feeling, like I'd let it slip through my fingers.

"It's okay," I mumbled. I stared at her swollen ankles bulging out of her knitted slippers. I wanted her to leave me alone. She lifted one hand. A stone turtle rested in the other. She petted it.

"I shouldn't have let her go."

Who? Who was this now? Why couldn't she go work on

her cutouts? Why couldn't she throw out all this junk? Why was she petting a fake turtle?

"That day they came and took her back. She was still a little girl. But I couldn't get her to eat. Couldn't get her to sleep. After a while, I couldn't do any of it anymore."

My mother? Was that who she was talking about? I didn't want to hear it. It wouldn't bring her back.

"Kids do that," I said bitterly. "They have bad dreams and their stomachs hurt. What did you expect?" I pictured Carla's orphans, sitting in the dirt, gobbling down their lunches, devouring every crumb, not one of them barfing.

"That social services woman says it happens sometimes. Your mother didn't cry when she was led to that woman's car. She didn't even look back. It was my greatest shame."

"You shouldn't have got her if you didn't plan to keep her." It's not right. Giving something. Taking it back.

Grandma pulled a Kleenex out of her housecoat pocket and sniffed and squeezed and blew. Her other hand cradled the turtle.

"Why did you?"

"You can't understand, Joey."

I wanted to slap her puffy cheek. If I couldn't understand, why did she bring it up?

"The Shore girls were everything to me. They were my life. Little Elizabeth. She was so precious. When Albert sent me away, I didn't know what to do. I'd been with those girls every day since — since their mother died. And then Albert barred me from the house. There were children with special needs who needed good homes. I heard about it on a radio program. On the CBC. So I phoned the social services."

Grandma must have thought, why not, trade one little girl for another. But then she got Carla, who was already wrecked, who wanted to sleep in a closet on a pile of shoes and hide bits of food under the rug.

"I wanted to help," Grandma was saying. "I thought I could provide a good home. I won't turn you away, Joey. You can be cross. I won't turn you away."

"Whatever." I moved around her standing there in the junk of the living room and stumbled towards the door. "It doesn't matter. She's gonna come back." Grandma called my name, but I kicked open the screen and ran.

* * *

At suppertime I pushed peas around my plate with my fork. Grandma was staring at me with her fat face, so I stood up quickly and offered to wash the dishes instead of just drying them.

I was scrubbing the crusties off the frying pan when Melvin Peevley stopped by with the weekly grocery order. He hoisted the paper bags onto the kitchen table and sat down beside Grandma. I stood at the sink with my back to both of them.

"How's the boy making out?" he asked Grandma, as if I wasn't right there.

I stared at their square reflections in the kitchen window. Grandma counted bills from the little purse around her neck and passed them to Melvin. Wisps of her hair stuck up every which way. Melvin's ponytail dangled like a dead rat. He smelled like sausage. They chatted about blueberries and bagging deer and about the coffee house at the LetterDrop, how the whole town takes a whirl at the karaoke mic and then everyone gets carrot cake. Grandma asked about some guy with a fiddle, and Melvin said, he's dead, remember, he'd brought her the program, and then he listed the people who went to the guy's funeral. I held the potato knife and stabbed at my fingertip under the suds. I thought about the similarities between wrists and antlers, about sawing them off, and which would be harder.

But then Melvin was blabbering about how the girl didn't seem to need much. What girl? I whirled around, flinging bubble strings across the counter.

"I said I'd deliver her groceries," he was telling Grandma. "Told her it would be no extra trouble. But she won't have it. Got a steely look, that girl."

Grandma had her mouth pursed in a wrinkled frown.

"We were hoping you might know something, Nelda. Like what's going on over there."

I plunked down in the only chair between them.

Melvin looked at me with concern. "What'd you do to your face, son?"

I blurted, "Did you see her?" A pinprick of watery blood fell on the table. I swiped my wet hands on my jeans, smearing pink.

"Well she's gone, Joey."

"Rebee. Gone?" I fought the cramps, clamping my jaw shut.

Melvin shook his head like I was an idiot. "Not Rebee. I was just over there. It's her mother who's gone."

"You talked to her? When?" I wanted to ram him with my fists. Why could he be the one?

"Just a jiffy ago. Before I came here." Then he laughed,

pleased with himself, and winked at Grandma. "Your boy here is a lovesick bull."

I pushed away from the table and flailed my way to my room. My eyes watered. Baby's tears. I tried to fight them back but they wouldn't stop coming. I could still smell her, still feel her body pressed against my thudding chest. Why wouldn't she talk to me? Why wouldn't she come to her door when it was me standing on the other side? I had been banned like the others. Like the Judge banned the old woman. Like the old woman banned my mother. Like my mother banned me. All that hurt. All that pathetic seeping hurt going round and round.

Melvin eventually said his goodbyes.

Grandma eventually got herself into bed.

I eventually padded down the hallway and knocked on her door. My stomach was eating me from the inside out, hissy and burning.

"Who's that?"

"Me, Grandma."

"Joey?"

I'd never been in her bedroom. It was surprisingly neat, no junk stacks floor to roof, front to back. Everything was pink. Pink bedspread, pink lampshades, pink doilies, pink poodle dolls. She lay like a giant creampuff in a sea of pink pillows. She squinted as I got closer, the light from the hallway creeping in with me.

"What is it, Joey. Did you have a bad dream?"

"Grandma, I need to ask you something."

"What, dear?" I sat down beside her on the sagging bed.

"Why did the Judge ban you from his house?"

"Joey."

"Please."

She patted her hand along her night side table, stalling. Her glasses were beside her Kleenex box. I reached over and passed them to her and sat on her bed. In the dim light, pink from the pillows splashed colour across her leathery cheeks. I waited. We both just stared at each other.

"I knew too much," she said finally. "That was all, Joey. That was my crime."

"Too much about what?"

"About the Judge."

Maybe that was my crime too. Maybe I knew too much. I knew her smell. I knew the shape of her. I knew that she used to dream about a daddy. That her real daddy was dead. That she waited by the side of the road for her mother to wake up. That she was not unbreakable, even though she looked at you with those fierce warrior eyes.

Grandma said something.

"What?" I leaned in closer.

"Not Albert. The other one."

The other one? "Two judges?"

"Oh, yes. There were two. William Sacks. A circuit judge as well. Albert's peer, but much younger. I met him, only the once. He was too glib, too handsome, too smartly put together for his own good. He wore that gold watch on a chain in his vest pocket, something an older man would choose. He kept taking that watch out, opening it up, snapping it closed again, as though time flew by for an important man like him. I didn't like the look of him."

Grandma was trying to sit up, breathing in short little breaths. I propped another pillow behind her back.

"So what about him?"

"It was so long ago, Joey."

"Please, Grandma. It's important." I didn't know why, but it was.

She looked haggard, worn out, blinking behind her splotchy glasses into the light of the hallway. "There had been only the one time — just that one time when Albert went to Edmonton for the Damer boy trial. William came to the house. He was fully aware that Albert was gone. Elizabeth put Victoria to bed. She and William drank brandy in front of the fire. She didn't stop him."

Didn't stop him from what?

Oh. This was awkward.

Grandma eyed me warily, like she wasn't sure she should go on. "Do you know about girls, Joey?"

Jesus. "I know they don't lay eggs, Grandma. So, what happened?"

A long pause. "When she started to show, Elizabeth couldn't bear it. She told Albert everything. I warned her not to, but she wouldn't listen. Such yelling in that house after that." Grandma pulled a Kleenex out from somewhere beneath the blankets and wiped at her nose. "And then, of course, Elizabeth died. So suddenly. And then nothing could be done to make it right for either one of them. Albert let it eat away at him, until he forgot how much he once loved her."

What a picnic, growing up in that house. No wonder the Shore sisters weren't that eager to stick around. Maybe that's why the Judge offed himself. A little after the fact, but still. . .

"So what about the other judge?" I asked. Rebee's real grandfather. The man with the pocket watch. "Did he come back? Did he want Harmony?"

"Harmony?"

"The baby. Did he try to get the baby?"

"No. No. Nothing like that. But Albert still had to work with him. Bad business, that was. I don't know why he didn't just give up on judging and take up something else."

He was still out there somewhere. Rebee's grandpa. William Sacks. Maybe Rebee ran into him at a fruit stand and didn't even know.

Grandma reached towards the nightstand for her half-filled glass and I passed it to her and she sipped on her water. "He's long dead now. Years ago. It was all over the radio. Killed by a runaway car. Late in the night, right in front of his house. He and his apple tree knocked to the ground. He didn't die instantly. He lay on the ground for a long time, and if someone had found him, he might have been saved. It was like that driver was sitting there waiting for him."

"That's gross," I said, a pinecone in my belly, its layers scraping my insides. "Who did it?"

"Someone he'd sentenced most likely. That's what the radio said. Judges have many enemies."

I could hear rumblings from under her pink blankets.

"Oh dear, I have to visit the bathroom."

I pulled her blanket away from her. A bad egg smell rose up. Grandma slid one massive leg across the sheets and let it fall to the floor. Then the other. I tucked my hands under her jiggling elbow and heaved till she was up and moving.

I held onto her until we got to the hall. Then I watched her feel her way unsteadily past the boxes piled floor to ceiling, past the detergent drums and newspaper stacks. When she got to the bathroom door, she turned back to me and said, "The gossips in this town know nothing, Joey."

* * *

I dreamed bad dreams. I dreamed we were driving on a highway that dropped into a bottomless hole. The car was greasy with fingerprints. Rebee had no clothes, she was bare everywhere, the kind of fantasy I would gladly work myself into a frenzy over, except her body was blistering and char-broiled and her breasts were black and hanging, nothing like the way she is, and my seatbelt wouldn't pry loose no matter how hard I yanked, and Carla popped up from the backseat and dangled a pocket watch in my face and whispered slobbery in my ear, *What did I tell you, Joey, what did I tell you.* I stumbled into the bathroom and kneeled in front of the toilet until my knees turned blue.

* * *

Grandma looked off balance when I came into the kitchen the next morning. She'd forgotten to take her curlers out. Her apron hung lopsided around her huge middle.

"Did you sleep well, Joey?"

I nodded.

"Good," she said, lifting muffins from the tin. They dropped to the counter like rocks.

It was possibly the worst night ever, except maybe that time when Carla crawled home with that sicko from the bar, and he sat on the couch and swatted at the *terrible angel* coming out of the TV.

"The happy pills must be working," Grandma was saying.

What was I? Three? "I'm going out to get some fresh air."

She wrapped my muffins in a paper towel and kissed me

on the cheek. "Take these. And don't play near the road."

I wandered over to the drop-off back of our houses and chucked the muffins one at a time into the forest below. I thought about that mess over at the Shore house, the stuff Rebee inherited. About her grandpa who wasn't. Her missing mom. It wasn't those details that were hard to understand. I had a grandma who wasn't. My mom was missing too. What I couldn't figure out is why Rebee was avoiding me. I thought about her pressed against me in that car. Everything about it had felt good, even my stomach. Why couldn't we just stay like that?

I spotted her backpack first, then the rest of her. She was zigzagging her way down the steep hill, as sure-footed as a mountain goat.

"Rebee," I yelled. "Rebee. Wait." For one happy second I thought everything would be right again.

"It's me. Joey." I waved my arms wildly. We could sit on the moss and Rebee could lean on me and talk about whatever she wanted and maybe I'd make her laugh and my gut would stop rolling.

But she just stared back as if she didn't know me. She looked through me as if I'd already been erased. Then she turned away and hitched her heavy pack up high on her shoulders and headed down the hill.

¥ ¥ ¥

I wandered up and down Chesterfield's streets. Pointlessly. Nobody was around; the whole town was someplace else, someplace they were meant to be. Before this morning, I'd imagined killing someone with my bare hands just to be able to see Rebee again. But then she looked up at me through the trees, and her eyes were dead, and she couldn't see me. I was nothing. I was a toilet that kept overflowing. I was a stupid dweeb she leaned against in a car. A pillow of bones.

I hated her. I hated her with my whole heart. Grit blew in my eyes. Grit blew the Sugarbowl right in front of me. That girl opened the window and leaned out on dirty elbows.

"Where you bin? Whoa, Tiger, you in a fight?"

I shrugged. Tiny roads of red crisscrossed her painted eyes. Her apron was filthy. "Up there on Blueberry Hill. Having a grand time, are ya? Cone?"

She spun around in her dingy shack and bent over the giant tubs. Purple strings from her ratty panties rode up in a V from her butt crack. She plunked the blob hard on the cone, chipping the edge, then licked her fingers and smacked her lips and twirled around and held out her arm.

"Well, take it," she said, pushing the cone in my face.

I stared at her flaked nails, yellowed holes under black paint. Little swirls of dust jumped off the street.

"What? You seen a ghost or somethin'?"

The image of Rebee swam through me, the dream Rebee. Dangling, black breasts, an empty look on her face, like I was a bug too small to see.

"The Judge left a car," I told her. I said it slowly, my voice a whispered crack. I nearly backed down. But I didn't. "Nobody knows. It's not locked."

It took her a full minute to get the drift. Then she squinted her eyes and snorted, slapping her hand hard on her hip. Her red eyes twinkled, some dark twisted thing in her smile.

"Omigod. You're not half stupid, Tiger."

I left her holding the cone and walked away.

⁎ ⁎ ⁎

I was a stone turtle, arms and legs tucked under my chest. Sometimes being a turtle put a lid on the cramps. I was lying like that, my head buried in the sheets, when the cars came up the hill.

I felt a terrible dread. When Carla's bar buddies used to come sniffing round, pissed up and itchy for trouble, I stayed invisible, usually in my closet. But this was my fault. I pulled on my hoody, climbed out my window and crept along the hedge under a thousand bright stars. In Rebee's front yard, big, sweaty bodies piled out of two cars. Ripped jeans and motorcycle boots and chains hanging. Five guys, two girls it looked at first, but then Sugarbowl girl popped up from behind one of the beefed-up greasers. She threw her head backwards and leaned into the crook of his arm and he poured a bottle down her throat. She glugged and sputtered and bent over laughing, swiping her mouth with the back of her hand. Bodies shuffled, shushing each other, laughing hysterically, heads bobbing up and down, weaving and swaying. They were crazy drunk. Rebee's house was utterly dark. Curtains closed. I hoped to God she was in a coma; that she'd stay that way 'til it was over.

I crawled out from behind the hedge and ran through an open patch of dirt, while the stars shone a bullseye on my head, *free geek, come get him*. But no one spotted me, so I hid behind a tree.

They formed a circle in front of Rebee's house. Even from behind that tree, the stink of booze was so heady I couldn't breathe.

They stumbled around and then the guys went off at

once. *HELLOOOOO. Beeeeeeeee afraid. I'm completely dead. I've come to drink your blood. WAAAAAAH. I'm the asshole Judge and I've come to —*

"Stop it," the girl with the sparkly glove whined. "It's creepy enough up here."

More ooooohing and aaaaahing.

"Forget the fucking ghosts," boomed the big one with ice cream girl attached to his hip. "Car, remember."

Ice cream girl slapped his cheek. "You're such a dipshit, JD."

He lurched forward, pushing ice cream girl back, and yelled, "So where is it? This car you been beaking off about? The '59 Caddy. That asshole loved his car."

They passed the bottle, blubs and glugs. A guy lit a pipe, and sent it round the circle. A crumbled pack of Marlboros whizzed through the air. A click of Bics, flashes of fire.

The shaved head guy said, "Maybe we should have ourselves a little bonfire. Burn the creep's place down."

I crouched on the ground in my hiding spot behind the tree. What had I done? I felt too sick to be sick, dizzy and bloodless.

The greasers hooted and hollered. *For sure. Absofuckingtootly. Burn the house down.* The girls hugged themselves. They didn't know I was there.

Ice cream girl piped up, "You burn his house down, you stay in jail for sure this time." She stamped her foot and her cigarette dropped from her mouth.

My heart lubbed in my chest. I felt like crumpling. Only now they were moving towards her door. What if they really did burn down her house? What if Rebee was inside and couldn't get out? What if she was crouched behind a window, scared out of her skull?

I tried to stop my feet, begged them to stay still, but they wouldn't listen. I picked myself up, pieces of me, and stepped out from behind the tree.

"Wait," I sputtered.

Ice cream girl spotted me first. She stumbled over and fell into me, a giggle and whoosh. "Tiger. Tiger. Buddy. LUUUUV you." She pulled-pushed me towards the others.

The JD guy loomed right in front of me. He seemed to be the one in charge.

"You the kid next door?" he said.

I kept my eyes down, not daring to look. The others bunched behind, except for the Kiss T-shirt guy, who muttered something about taking a leak. He wandered round the side of the house, back to where the Judge's rotting garage tilted on the cliff.

Ice cream girl crashed into JD and slid down his arm. He grabbed a wad of blue hair and yanked her back up.

"Tell 'bout the car, Tiger," she slurred. "Asshole Judge." Black streaks ran down her cheeks. She tried to point at me, but she couldn't hold her finger steady, doodling wildly in the air.

Rebee's dark porch breathed at my back. "There is no car." My heart stopped.

"Really," JD snorted, blowing smoke in my face. "Thas not what you told Jemma here." He steered her around to face me.

I swallowed. Did not take a breath. "There is no car. I made the story up."

Her name was Jemma. She couldn't stay upright. JD let go and she thudded to the ground. The not pretty girl with the square face tripped over her, but righted herself before she fell down. "Let's get out of here," she said, stumbling towards JD. "This place creeps me out."

Shaved head said, "We're gonna go in. Check things out. See where the Judge did the dirty deed." They all laughed. Except JD.

The sparkly-gloved girl hugged her arms and rocked back and forth. "We can't go in there. He's in that house."

"So's Elvis," someone yelled from behind.

"No. Really. I can feel him. Let's go, 'kay?"

JD flicked his arm. "Shut up already." Everybody shut up. Jemma groaned on the ground. JD's whole mad-drunk concentration landed on me. "So what about the car, kid?"

I looked down, catching a glimpse of his belt buckle, and swallowed.

"Well?"

I shook my head. "I made it up. About the car. The Judge sold it to a car dealer in Edmonton. Before he died. Melvin Peevley said so. Ask him yourself. At the LetterDrop."

The others went quiet.

"The Judge would never a sold that car," JD said.

I couldn't think of anything else to convince him.

"You lie to all your friends?" he asked this friendly-like, just a nice simple question. "Well?" He grabbed a fistful of my hoody and pulled me into him. I dangled under his chin in front of the constellations and gulped mouthfuls of leaking booze and oniony sweat and a sour smell like my sheets after a bad night. If JD let go in that second, I'd fall on my face. But he didn't. I stayed pinned to his hand, while he contemplated what to do next. I flashed through the possibilities, the parts of me he would hurt first. I thought about how long I'd last until I cried like a baby. My heart hammered against my skin.

I was about to pee myself. But then she was there. No one knew how. She just floated from the shadows of the porch and landed right beside me.

"Jesus," JD flung his fingers wide, freeing me in an instant. He fumbled backwards. "Jesus." He panted a little, blinking. The others, too. Sparkly glove covered her mouth. Jemma got on all fours and then climbed herself up off the ground, bracing herself against square face.

The goons huddled together, all bluster gone. They stared wide-eyed at the ghost of the girl in front of them. I stared, too. Had she swum out of my head? Nothing about her looked real. The whites of her unblinking eyes were piercingly bright. She had a wild, warrior look, almost electric. The slivered moon washed over her, skin deathly pale, blue tinged. She wore no shoes, her bare toes planted wide, hands at her side, perfectly still. Fearless.

"Who the hell are you?" JD wanted to know.

She stared at JD so fiercely he had to look away. He groped his pockets for cigarettes, then a match. It took him three tries to get the thing lit.

"You're on my property," Rebee said.

He shrugged to the others, as if, look, it's only a girl. "Your property," he snorted. "This is the Judge's place."

"So you don't belong here."

"And you do?"

"Yes."

"You a relation or sumthin'? He's dead. This place was supposed to be empty."

Rebee didn't answer.

"The Judge was a friend of ours." JD grinned to the others standing behind him. "We're gonna take a look-see is all.

Make sure his old Caddy is doing okay."

Nobody else made a sound.

"There's nothing to see," Rebee said, as if she believed it.

"You say."

"I do."

"I'm sorry, Rebee," I whispered. I wanted to get us inside and barricade the door. But she stood her ground.

Then there was a commotion around the side of the house. The greaser who'd gone off to piss in the trees came back into sight. "JD, come see," he yelled. "There's an old garage back there." And then, "Holy shit! Who's she?"

Rebee didn't bother to look his way. Her eyes stayed on JD. "Like I said," she told him. "There is no car."

"But there's a garage," JD said.

"Apparently."

"That Caddy inside, all dressed up, nowhere to go?"

Rebee didn't blink.

"If there's no car, you won't mind if we go see."

She narrowed her eyes and took a long, slow, deep breath. "All right. I'll show you the way. And then you and your little friends can get off my property."

She glided away from us. JD was pissed, eyes glaring. He wasn't used to this kind of girl. He stomped off after her, his drunken groupies following.

"Rebee," I called out, my guts rising as I stumbled to keep up. She couldn't have forgotten what was behind that door. I'd spent the best night of my life inside that car. What was she planning to do? Twitch her nose, make it disappear?

I could feel the earth biting her bare feet as my runners tripped along beside her. It was a long trek, farther than I remembered. The stars tracked us across the clearing. That sorry building loomed closer and closer.

"I'm sorry, Rebee," I stammered. The others rustled and crunched behind us like rats. What would JD do to her?

Too soon we were in front of the garage door. Rebee stood, legs apart, hands on her hips. There was no place to hide. I stood beside her.

She turned and faced the pack. "Here we are," she said casually.

JD licked his lips. "Here we are." That big, stupid greaser wanted to slide in behind the wheel like he was king of the hill, stomp his foot on the pedal, gun the engine, squeal out of there. Rebee couldn't stop it. She'd try. And she'd get hurt. She'd get hurt bad cause of me.

"Go ahead," Rebee said, pointing to the door. "Open it."

JD stepped forward, puffing himself up like a peacock. He bent at the waist and grabbed hold of the rusted handle, twisting around slowly to glint at the others. The door cracked open a few inches, releasing a musty smell.

My insides roared, my fear stink wrestling with all the other bad smells. JD was yanking the curved metal of the handle, his body bent in two right in front of me. He moved in slow motion, like he had nothing but time. I didn't. I only had a second before the whole world fell apart. *Open the door, JD. See the shiny car. See Joey run.*

Everything bad in me needed to get out. I hadn't done a single right thing in my small pathetic life. I was good for nothing. I had one and only one skill. I didn't so much think it, as become it. I opened my mouth, clenched my gut muscles, and summoned up great mounds of vomit. JD was on his way up, coming out of his crouch. I *blaached* everything I had at him. It landed on his belt buckle, dripped off the swell of his gut, splattered along the thighs of his jeans, coated his outspread arms.

"Jesus," he cried, staggering backwards into the pack. Rebee stood motionless. The others yowled and scattered. JD stared down at himself, at the globs dripping off him. My globs.

"I'm gonna kill you, you little puke," he snarled, flinging his head, a mad dog.

Rebee stepped closer to me. "You wanted a look-see. Here you go." She tugged at the door ferociously until it groaned all the way up. I blinked the water from my eyes, waiting for the Cadillac to come out of the shadows. But there was just a black empty nothingness.

"Satisfied?" Rebee said calmly, brandishing her arm like a magician. The smell didn't seem to faze her.

JD stared into the gaping empty hole beyond the door, his jaw hanging open, his rage extinguished.

The others were done with this party. They slunk back through the clearing in twos and threes, arguing about who would ride with JD.

"So you can get off my property now," Rebee said to JD.

He glowered from me to Rebee to his disappearing buddies and then back to me. His fist clenched against his nose. He reeked. What was he thinking? *I can ignore it, beat the crap out of this puker.* I inched backwards into the empty garage.

"You really want to do this?" Rebee asked, her voice low. She stepped towards JD. "Your friends are leaving."

He glared after his retreating buddies. "That kid puked all over me," he growled.

"I know," Rebee responded. "He does that when he's scared."

And when he's happy and when he's bored, I wanted to tell her. But she was right. He does that when he's scared. Mostly.

"You just wanted to take a look was all," Rebee was saying, so quiet she was almost whispering.

"So whad he do with it?" JD had toned it down considerably.

"Go, JD. If it turns up, you can have it."

"Yah, sure."

"Really," she said. "I don't want it."

He looked like he could almost believe her if she just kept talking in that calming voice.

"Go JD. There's nothing you want here tonight."

Miraculously, he went. Slowly, at first. One clumsy backwards step at a time, not taking his eyes off her. Then he turned and stomped towards the others, the stink going with him. Drunk talk. Yelling. Doors slamming. The ground vibrating with the boom, boom, boom of cranked stereos and engines. Tires spun on the loose gravel.

And then we were alone in the night, Rebee and me. I crept out of my hiding place and stood beside her. What do you say after something like that?

"Hi, Rebee," I said.

She looked up at the stars. So much light reflected in her eyes. We were mere specks under the twinkling sky. It felt like we were the only ones left to breathe for the world.

Rebee took a deep gulp of air, filling her lungs. "It's nice here," she said quietly.

"Rebee, I'm sorry that I — "

But she was moving away. Again. Striding forwards, into the clearing. It seemed if we weren't in a car, I spent all my time scrambling behind her.

"Rebee. I'm trying to tell you. I brought them here. Oh purpose. To stir up trouble. Trouble for you. On purpose!"

She dropped down in a grassy patch by some overgrown bushes. She lay on her back, spread her arms wide, and stared up at the sky. Of course I'd seen this before. That first time, from my hedge spot. The next kazillion times, she did her lying-down thing in my head. Rebee under the sky. Rebee under my skin. The pictures looked the same. I loved looking at them. I loved looking at her.

"I'm trying to apologize." I stood over her, feeling hot and fired up. "You're not even listening."

"Lie down beside me. Look up."

"Don't you care I brought them here?" I said, my voice too loud, echoing a little. "JD could have punched you. I bet he punches girls all the time. This whole stupid night was my fault."

Rebee pulled one knee up and swayed it back and forth. She kneaded her toes in the tall grass. "It's not so stupid. Look."

I felt like a human blender. My body ached all over. I didn't want to look up, or look down on her like a moron, so I plunked on my ass and flattened myself in the grass. "Where did the car go?" I asked, eyes closed.

"It's gone," Rebee said.

"Gone where?"

"I got rid of it. I didn't want it here."

Got rid of it? Just like that? "So who did you call?" A tow truck? Mr. Melvin I-Can-Do-Anything?

"No one."

"You said you couldn't drive."

"I underestimated myself."

"Oh." I was afraid to open my eyes. I was afraid to think about what she'd done. Did she get rid of everything she didn't want? Cars, mothers, crazy aunties, drunken grease balls, zit boys from next door?

"Open your eyes, Joey. Look for a shooting star."

It was incredible. The big night sky hurtling down. Blue-white points, reds and yellows, round fuzz balls, light bouncing. It was better than a movie.

We lay like that for a long time, side by side on the grass. There was a kids' song about falling stars, but I couldn't think of the words. Rebee spotted two, one right after the other. I missed them both.

"How come you were ignoring me?" I asked. "That's why I told Jemma about the car. I was mad at you. I knew she'd tell her hoser friends."

"People do bad things," Rebee said, too matter-of-factly. Then she passed me her Wintergreen package. I wanted to ask, what people? Did she mean me, or her, or JD, or the world? But she said, "Un-focus your eyes. Look for different shapes in the patterns."

I saw floaters more than shapes. I took a Life Saver and gave her back the roll.

"I thought I hated you," I said.

"Do you?"

"No. Of course not."

She pointed to the tiny lights above us. "Makes you want to reach up and grab one."

I wanted to take her hand. "Are we friends?" I held my breath.

She stayed quiet for too long, so I asked again. "Are we, Rebee?"

Rebee cupped her hands behind her head. She still wasn't looking at me. "You don't need a friend like me, Joey."

I leaned on my elbow and stared at her. Her eyes were enormous. Strands of her hair shimmered silver under the stars. "Yes, I do," I said. "Is it cause I'm a dweeb?"

She sat up and brushed grass off her sweater. "Stop feeling sorry for yourself. You're quite brave really. And you've got perfect aim."

"Brave," I snorted. "I'm the biggest coward I know."

"I watched you behind that tree."

"You saw that? Me?"

"Uh-huh," she said.

Of course she could see that dweeby stick of a boy sniveling behind a tree. She was a girl who saw everything.

"You could have stayed there," she stretched her arms. "But you didn't."

"And you think that's brave?"

"I do."

She didn't say things just to be nice. She really meant it. "Then why can't we be friends?"

"All right," she said, finally. "For tonight we're friends."

"I don't want to be friends just for tonight." I was whining like a baby, but I couldn't help myself.

Rebee sighed. "You're hard to please."

"Don't you care what happens?" My heart was thudding.

She was remarkably calm. Annoyed maybe. "We'll call this whatever you want. Your mom will come back. Soon, I bet. You'll get settled in school somewhere and you'll meet real friends and you'll forget all about Chesterfield and this crazy summer."

She was ready to end it before we even started. She

thought she knew me, but she was wrong. I didn't want other friends. I wanted her. I didn't care if Carla ever showed up. In fact, I'd rather she didn't.

"My mom's nuts. I never want to see her again."

Rebee turned to me under that big shining sky. "Listen to me. Your mom comes back, you go with her. Eat your Cheerios. Do your math. You watch and listen. Endure. One day, it will be over. You'll wake up one morning and realize you can walk out that door and take any road you want." She put her fingers on my shoulder and squeezed. "You don't have to end like you started, Joey. You know that, right?"

I didn't know anything. All I wanted was to stay with her on the grass. But she was getting to her feet, stretching her arms slow and strong. She took my arm and pulled me to my feet and towards the hedge that separated our houses. I limped along beside her silently. When we got to the road, she said, "You'll be okay, Joey."

"Whatever."

How could I tell her? I was thirteen. She was more than I knew how to imagine.

She fished her Wintergreens from her jeans pocket and took my hand in hers. She dropped the roll in my palm and closed my fist in her fingers and held them there. Her skin felt warm, hot almost. "In case you need light," she said, smiling.

I watched until she got halfway to her porch. Then I yelled, "Don't ignore me, Rebee."

"I won't," she said with a wave of her arm. She might have been lying, telling me what I needed to hear, because even though I chanted in my head, *look back*, *look back*, *look back*, she never did.

* * *

Rebee got it part right.

Carla showed up the next morning to collect me like I was a box waiting for her at the post office. She arrived at ten. By half past eleven we were careening down the highway. I couldn't stop us. It started lovey-dovey. Joey, baby, look at you. What happened to your forehead? Give your momma a hug. So great of you to watch him for me, Nelda.

Let's make nice didn't last. It never does with Carla. She can't keep her mouth shut. Shouldn't you get rid of this, Nelda? What are you saving that old thing for? Grandma skulked around in her knitted slippers, slamming cupboards, muttering about how the girl was ungrateful, so high and mighty you'd think she'd just hung the moon. I thought she'd be an ally, but by the time Carla was done, Grandma seemed ready to be rid of us both.

I stayed away from Rebee's door. I didn't want goodbyes. Rebee knew a lot of stuff, but she didn't know everything. She didn't know, for example, that you can rearrange your existence so as not to forget. Every thought, every movement, every feeling, every molecule. Your survival can depend on it.

Carla said she'd borrowed the car from her new friend. Calvin somebody or other. It smelled like dirty feet. A pair of scuffed handcuffs dangled from the rear-view mirror. She'd brought me a stupid beaded basket, courtesy of her orphan boys. Either my mother had really managed to get herself to Africa, or the basket was a cover from the dollar store. She hadn't brought up Jesus once. She coulda spent the summer in Vegas for all I knew.

Carla waited until her first pee break before she thought to ask, "Anything go on for you? While I was gone?"

Nothing, Carla. Nothing at all.

There was stomach thunder, the start of the threat. I fingered Rebee's Life Savers, wedged in my pocket. I concentrated on rearranging my insides. Rebee in the grass. Rebee in me. My guts tried to push her out, but she was too strong, and when the shredded strands shrank back to their cave, I was covered in sweat and feeling like I'd won something.

Carla parked at a rest stop beside an overflowing garbage can. The sign said no camping like somebody might. There was a sagging wooden picnic table with shattered boards along the top. A group of brown cows bunched by a fence behind the outhouses.

"Aren't you getting out?" She rummaged through her purse, pulled out her lipstick, and smeared red across her mouth.

"Stop sulking, Joey. I came back, didn't I?" When I didn't answer, she slammed her door hard.

The cows raised their heads. We stared at each other until one by one they shoved their noses back in the tall grass. I closed my eyes, waiting for Carla to finish her business, and endured.

REBEE

SOMETIMES I THINK ABOUT DROWNING. I see myself standing on the cliff looking down. Darkness falls, and the water below churns and roars. The Judge's car starts to rise from the bottom of the troubled lake, and my fear rises with it. I tell myself that nobody knows; there will be no search. I tell myself all kinds of lies to make the trembling stop.

* * *

Sometimes I think about those ice children discovered in the mountains of the ancient Inca Empire. And the others, too. The ones who haven't been found, sacrificed to the mountain gods by their mothers. Children buried close to heaven with nothing but bags of nail clippings their mothers saved for them in case their spirits returned.

Nail clippings are necessary in uncivilized times. When Jake came to my grandfather's house that day,

I flushed mine down the toilet. I just opened my nail box and sprinkled them into the water. I suppose I decided, without really thinking it, there was nothing left of that world to hang onto.

I don't need nails to keep me safe anymore. I've learned to wear mittens in January. To shield my July eyes from the white hot sun. To sleep without dreaming, to wake without fighting my pillow.

I've learned to cook too. Carrots in orange sauce. Asparagus with lemon. Sticky rice. Apple pie. I cook roasts on Sundays in my grandfather's blue-speckled pot, opening my closets and drawers, letting the dark meaty smell get into my sweaters and shoes. This weekend, I'm going to bake the Chocolate Angel Food Cake, page 292 from *County Cooking*, with powdered sugar and frosting daisies and twenty-one candles circling the top.

My mother forgot to teach me these things. That's not true. My mother forgets nothing.

I don't even know how to find her. Vanishing is what she does best. Over and over and over again. We never left Alberta, ricocheting inside her borders like an angry bullet. Just look at her map, shaped like a holster. If you look closely, you can find the dot named Chesterfield. Inside the dot, look for Blueberry Hill. Step around the towering hedge that no one owns and out onto the oiled road. When you can go no further, you can see the white house with the stippled green roof, the wrap-around veranda and the old wicker chair.

This is the place where my mother lived. She lived with the Judge, the man who lies buried in the sixth row of the Chesterfield cemetery on the far side of the dot. You can search for what she will not forget in this house. Search in the closets, the bed sheets, the desk drawers with the brass handles. You won't find any evidence. Before I came here, I searched in the silence as we flitted like moths atop the pimply dots of the holster. I searched and searched, trying to sniff out our history in her green-grey eyes, in the smells along the highway, in the night words she whimpered from her mattress on the floor.

Before I even knew of this place, I wanted to know if her leaving it — her running — had something to do with me.

It did, of course. But it doesn't matter anymore. I can tell you now that I'm all grown up, that I don't need a mother to keep me safe. That might be a lie. Sometimes, in the middle of the night, I stand at her window, and I think I see her haunted eyes staring back at me. And I have to remind myself that it's not really my fault. That I am me. And I have come home.

* * *

I was sixteen when I found this place. Aunt Vic and Harmony had been summoned to Chesterfield after the Judge's funeral. I don't know who whispered what when my grandfather was lowered to the ground. All I know is I wanted to stay. "There's nothing for you here," Harmony kept saying. But there was everything I ever wanted here. My mother's house. My mother's town. My family's huge kitchen with rows and rows of cupboards. None of it could fit into the back of a van.

What surprised me most was that my mother fought at all. There were no tearful goodbyes before she drove away. We could have been strangers who met at a truck stop as

I walked her to the van. Vic yelled out the window as they backed down the driveway, "I'll give you three weeks before you beg us to get you outta here."

But then they were gone, and I was alone and angry and so upside-down homesick I couldn't breathe. If Harmony had come back for me that first summer — if she'd just barrelled up Blueberry Hill and honked the horn — I would have jumped in the van, lit an incense stick, and let her drive us in circles for another sixteen years. But she didn't come back. And I knew I needed to stay. My grandfather's car became such a distraction, the way it whispered in my ear, calling me to the highway, telling me I belonged out there, nowhere. So I waited until Chesterfield was sleeping. I eased the car down Blueberry Hill, terrified to be in the driver's seat, fingers gripping the steering wheel so tight I thought they might break. I crawled towards the back road that led to the trailhead. Then I followed the narrow twisting trail, up, up, up, the car lurching on the loose gravel. When I reached the cliff — the end of the road — I opened the door and fell onto the cold ground. It took a long time until I could breathe normally. Then I stood up, moved the gearshift to drive, and pushed with all my strength. The Judge's car, carrying my whole past, inched slowly towards the edge, then hurled down the bank and disappeared into the black water.

* * *

He is better at finding than my mother is hiding. Jake arrived when the leaves were starting to fall from the trees. It was near the end of my first summer, a few weeks after my night on the cliff. I recognized him instantly when he rang my bell. He was wearing blue jeans and a suit jacket over his white shirt and his hair was combed back and curling over his collar. I was flooded by memories, a thousand little details. Washing dishes in the river. Playing cards at the picnic table. Harmony laughing. The sticky feel of pine needles. The smell of clean, white snow.

We stood in front of each other awkwardly. He didn't take his eyes off me, concentrated, dark with questions.

"Jake. Kit Creek. Remember? You've changed. You look more like your mother now."

"Why are you here?" I leaned around him and looked towards his empty truck.

"I heard about the Judge. I wanted to know you're okay. Are you? Okay?"

I couldn't believe he was real.

"Can I come in?" he asked.

"Why?" I felt angry for no reason that made sense.

"I've driven a long way to get here."

"She's gone," I said.

His voice sounded weary. "I know. I came to see you."

I stepped back from the door and he followed, this man I barely knew. We went from standing awkwardly at the front door to standing awkwardly in the kitchen. I eventually plunked myself into a chair, and Jake pulled out another and sat down beside me. We stayed like that for a long while, neither of us saying anything.

"After we met at the campground I went to look for my brother." He leaned towards me, hands on his knees. He didn't try to touch me, although he could have, and I wouldn't have backed away. "His name's Matt. I went all the way to Mexico." Jake's skin was the colour of hayfields in late summer.

"But he didn't want to be found. So I made a place for him, in case he decided to come home. I built a house on his property, my property now I suppose. Along the way, I did a little search for you and your mom, too. It wasn't hard. I had your license plate number and a guy named Elroy who knows that kind of stuff."

I thought maybe we owed him something. Something that would be hard to pay.

But then Jake said, "I found Chesterfield easy enough and then 21 Blueberry Hill. I figured you and your mom would come home one day."

He had a worried look then, which made me feel glad at first. Then I just felt tired.

"I got to know your grandpa some," Jake was saying. "I came up here a few times. Before today. Your grandpa, he was — "

"He's dead. He killed himself. On my sixteenth birthday."

Jake sat perfectly still. His eyes had the same gold flecks buried inside grey that peered in the van window on that snowy night. "If I'd of known, I would of done something. Maybe I could have stopped it."

But he couldn't have stopped anything. This family's rage burned like a torch.

Jake stayed all afternoon. He said he had something to give me and went to his truck to fetch it. When he came back, he had a house in his arms. There were glued trees in its front yard. Painted shutters. A tiny basket of flowers beside the front door.

Jake set the house down on the kitchen table, folded

his arms, and rocked on his heels. He could hardly look at me. His cheeks were flushed as he stammered through his speech. "I know you're too old for dolls. But I got this for you. When you were at that campground."

"I was too old then." It was an ungrateful thing to say, but I was so caught off guard, and there was such hesitancy in his eyes. He had uncertainty written all over his face, and surprise as well, as though until precisely that moment he had known his way.

"You don't have to keep it," he said, unfolding his arms, readying to reach down and take it away.

"No," I said, touching his sleeve. "I'll keep it."

I've put the dollhouse in my grandfather's living room beside the stone fireplace. A house within a house. Sometimes I lie on the floor, leg crossed over a knee, and stare through the little shuttered windows. I pretend there's a family inside. A father like Jake. A mother who is beautiful like Harmony, only she listens and smiles. There's a grandpa, too. He comes from my dreams, not my dreams of the dead man in the casket, but of a grandpa who carried me in his arms when I pretended to be sleeping. Only the daughter is a mystery. No matter how many times I try to imagine her as a little girl, she's too old for her age, not a child at all.

Before he left that day, Jake pulled a purple address book from the inside pocket of his jacket. The book's cover has two little kittens with bows around their necks. Jake sat across from me, red-cheeked, head bent, pointing to the page with his phone number and a carefully written set of directions to his place.

He said, "Call me, Rebee. As often as you like. I'll pay your phone bill. Call every day if you want. Will you do that?"

The hope in his voice brought a lump to my throat that tasted like warm honey. I thought about what it would be like. I could stand at my window, the phone to my ear. I could tell him how to read a map upside down. The places a person could get lost in. Ways to be invisible.

But that's the thing, isn't it? Hope has soft edges. Only after does it cut you to shreds. When he found us at the campground, I was so bloated with it I thought I might burst. Mile after mile I thought about him, about the man named Jake, about the man who was my father. I pummelled Harmony with questions like fists, which was not like me at all. I had always kept my mouth shut. But I was obsessed. Jake opened a vein and I couldn't stop bleeding. Who was my father? Was he disappointed I was a girl? Did he hold me in his arms when I was a baby? Would we ever see Jake again? Couldn't we go see my father? Couldn't we even once?

Harmony confessed on a day that started like any other. I was thirteen, hungry, hoping for breakfast, coughing up leftovers from my newly scarred lungs. We were setting up in a new town and waiting for the bank to open, and I was worrying about not finding the school and not having indoor runners without grass stains or scuffs. The bank had glass walls, like smoky mirrors, the kind where you could see your reflection clearly, only shadows of bank people milling inside. Four or five others waited, Harmony first in line. I stood well back from the wall, by myself, under the lamp pole. An older man in a pinstriped suit stepped out of his car, crossed the street slowly, and stood near to me. He held his bankbook in his hand, almost dangled it in front of me, and he wouldn't stop staring me up and down. At first, I thought I'd done something stupid, like I'd chosen a don't-wait-here zone, or had my shirt inside-out. This was before I knew men had permission to look at girls that way. Certain girls. Girls that tumble out of rundown vans. Girls that stand under lampposts when they should be in school. I tried not to squirm or look at him. I wanted the bank to hurry and open, intent on shrinking to invisible. I focused past his face, far into the distance, traced the D in the Dairy Queen sign, unblinking, eyes watering.

I turned and caught Harmony's reflection in the mirrored wall. She was seeing the man seeing me, with eyes I didn't recognize. They held an expression of pain, raw and gaping, a deep, open sore. I would have run to her, but that look in her eyes flickered then died, almost instantly, so fleeting in fact that I've wondered since if I imagined it there.

Harmony pushed past the others, strode over to us and stood between me and the man, legs slightly parted, shoulders back. The man backed up a step, looking surprised at first, perhaps a bit sheepish, smaller somehow than when he had me to himself. Harmony stepped toward him, one step, close enough to brush his pinstripes. She didn't say a word. But he looked afraid then, really afraid, of what he found in her eyes.

Nothing else happened with the man. The bank opened in that moment, good morning, good morning, and the people shuffled in. The man crossed the street again, quickly this time, got back in his car and drove away. We drove away, too. When we got to the highway, I asked, so what about the bank, but Harmony didn't answer. She was driving too fast, and I pressed against the back of my seat and thought about how she might have killed that guy.

She told me, hours later, after we'd turned onto a back road that crumbled to a stop at the mouth of an old barn.

"I'll say this only once, Rebee. Then we will not discuss it again. His name was William Sacks. He was a circuit judge, like your grandfather."

"Who?" I asked, clueless.

"We saw each other in secret. I was just a town girl. A stupid girl with stars in her eyes. Then I got pregnant and we ended. He's dead. I want you to forget about him."

I couldn't breathe, my past pushing me under like a wave. "Did he meet me? Even once?"

"He didn't meet you. He didn't want you, Rebee."

"Did he even know I existed?"

She ignored me, cranking the steering wheel, spewing gravel as she turned us around.

"What about my grandfather? Why can't we go see him? Maybe he'd like to meet me."

"He didn't want you either."

"He could change his mind. If he meets me, I mean."

"Drop it, Rebee. I gave you what you asked for. William Sacks. Sperm. That's all he was to you."

But I couldn't drop it. He sat like a heavy lump at the back of my throat.

Having Jake in my kitchen brought back that choking feeling. He stared at me like I was fragile, like I was precious to him. I could not afford hope, sitting at my table, inviting me to share my life. I lied to him that day. I said sure, of course I would phone him sometimes, though I knew that I wouldn't. How could it work? He would hear my voice and think of her. And I would hear his voice and think of her.

I've not seen him again. He calls on my birthday, and at Christmas, and many times for no reason. In those first clunky conversations, the way he said my name made me think I wasn't real to him; that I was just an idea tangled up in his hopefulness. He would ask if I needed money, or if the shingles or porch railings or plumbing needed fixing, and should he come to Chesterfield to check things out. But it's different now. We can talk for a long time and it doesn't hurt at all. He never asks about Harmony. I can only hear his longing for her, too, in the empty seconds before we say our goodbyes.

* * *

Six newspaper articles and three letters to the editor tell the story. My father was struck on June 27 in front of his house in Edmonton. It was in the dead of night — a single moment is all it would take — somewhere between the hours of eleven and two. The police called it suspicious; one went so far as to give it a title. Deliberate homicide, vehicular manslaughter. A lawyer wrote about how more needed to be done to ensure safety for circuit judges, those pillars of the community who made such a lasting contribution to justice in this land. The driver's vehicle jumped the curb and struck the victim with tremendous force. "Unprecedented" force, even for a hit and run, one report said. His body was found at 5:27 AM by a neighbour heading out for a morning run. He had remained pinned through the night between the twisted branches of the large uprooted tree in his front yard. Collapsed lungs and internal bleeding stopped his heart. It took several hours. He was sixty-one years old. Glass shards were scattered about the lawn and street. Police expected considerable damage to the suspect's vehicle, including broken headlights and a dented front end. The police appealed to the public for help in finding the driver or the vehicle. There were several tips, but both seemed to have vanished.

Of course clippings in newspapers and law journals are just scattered bits. They don't really tell the story. There's no mention, for example, of a little girl alone on a motel bed, or of the mother who left her there.

Harmony doesn't know what I know. How could she? I was so small. I had no business remembering the smell in that sad room or that too-big bed or that flashing neon sign or that blood on her face. I was two years old and locked in that room. When she came back for me, we drove through the black night, the van's front end screeching and shaking.

William Sacks, the circuit judge, cut through this family like a knife.

We got a different van somewhere. My grandfather was a regular provider. Sometimes I'll lie on the Judge's bed and close my eyes and try to picture the man my grandfather might have been. How could he love his little daughter when she was not his own? He was a man too wounded to heal himself.

I imagine my mother, trying to please a father who can't bear to look at her, and pleasing a father who does. And I imagine a mother named Harmony who kept me before she finally left me to grow on my own; and a grandfather who gave me a home to grow in.

* * *

Joey will be here by Saturday. He'll barge through the door, halting before we collide, and we'll study each other, shyly at first, taking in the changes, his new height and filled-out shoulders, his fading scar on the clear, smooth skin of his forehead. And he'll lift me high and twirl me around, to prove to me how strong he's become, and when he puts me back down I will feel dizzy with the extraordinariness of it.

We'll walk down into the woods out back and sit on a moss-covered log, and Joey will take a flat piece of green grass between his thumbs and blow it like a foghorn. Something to the side will catch his eye, and it will be Harmony's Tree, charred and black, but we won't speak of it. We'll pluck Indian paintbrushes out of the rock and wrap them together with wild twine. In the afternoon, we'll drive to the cemetery in Joey's rickety car and place the flowers on their graves, the Judge and Mrs. Nielsen's.

When it's evening, after I've blown out my candles, Joey will prowl around the kitchen and get in the way and eat another piece of cake. Aunt Vic will call, to wish me a happy birthday, and she'll say her feet are killing her and her waitressing days are over. She'll tell me her psychic said she should get herself a bloodstone and a piece of hematite to ward against harm.

And Jake will call, too, because it's my birthday, and I will see his face soften when he thinks of her. And when he says goodbye, he says *love you*, and I say it back, and it's true.

When it's dark, after Joey and I have put away the dishes, we'll sit side by side on the porch and breathe in the smells of summer all around. Joey will pull out his Wintergreens from somewhere deep in the pocket of his baggy jeans. He will carefully unfold the crinkled wrapping and pass one to me before popping another between his lips.

We'll look up at the stars, and I'll see them as beacons lighting her dark road.

ACKNOWLEDGEMENTS

Thanks are due to the Alberta Foundation for the Arts and to the Brenda Strathern Writing Prize for financial assistance in completing this book. *Prairie Fire* published an earlier version of "Jake" and *CBC Anthology* produced a Rebee story for CBC Radio. Thank you to the editors.

With much gratitude to everyone at NeWest Press, especially Andrew Wilmot, designer Natalie Olsen, and my wise and gentle editor, Anne Nothof. My heartfelt thanks goes to Rosemary Nixon, Aritha van Herk, Nicole Markotić, Annabel Lyon and Eunice Scarfe for their inspiration and early encouragement. Special thanks to my writing buddies, Kari Strutt, Heather Ellwood, Michael Davie, Lisa Willemse, and Cathy Jewison, for keeping me at my desk. I owe so much to my parents, Irma and Louis, my dearest sisters, Judy and Brenda, and my forever friends, Brenda and Pat.

Deepest love and gratitude to Breanna and Megan, whose tender love fills me, to Craig, for being family in all good ways, and to Jim, for being what matters most.

FRAN KIMMEL was born and raised in Calgary, Alberta. After graduating from the University of Calgary with a degree in Sociology, she worked an eclectic mix of jobs including youth worker, career counsellor, proposal writer, and a ten-year stint as a VP for a career consulting firm. Fran's stories have appeared in literary journals across Canada and have twice been nominated for the Journey Prize. Fran currently lives in Lacombe with her husband and overly enthusiastic silver Lab. This is her first novel.